TITANIC: RELATIVE FATE

ALSO BY V. C. KING

Seven Sexy Tales of Terror

TITANIC: RELATIVE FATE

A NOVEL

V. C. KING

iUniverse, Inc.
New York Lincoln Shanghai

TITANIC: RELATIVE FATE

Copyright © 2008 by V. C. King

All rights reserved. No part of this book may be used or reproduced by any means, graphic, electronic, or mechanical, including photocopying, recording, taping or by any information storage retrieval system without the written permission of the publisher except in the case of brief quotations embodied in critical articles and reviews.

iUniverse books may be ordered through booksellers or by contacting:

iUniverse
2021 Pine Lake Road, Suite 100
Lincoln, NE 68512
www.iuniverse.com
1-800-Authors (1-800-288-4677)

Because of the dynamic nature of the Internet, any Web addresses or links contained in this book may have changed since publication and may no longer be valid.

This is a work of fiction. All of the characters, names, incidents, organizations, and dialogue in this novel are either the products of the author's imagination or are used fictitiously.

ISBN: 978-0-595-45961-2 (pbk)
ISBN: 978-0-595-70181-0 (cloth)
ISBN: 978-0-595-90261-3 (ebk)

Printed in the United States of America

For Richard, Mom, and George

The disaster was just due to a combination of circumstances that never occurred before and can never occur again. That may sound like a sweeping statement, yet it is a fact.

—Commander Charles Lightoller, *Titanic*'s second officer and the senior surviving officer, from his book *Titanic and Other Ships* (Ivor Nicholson & Watson, 1935)

Acknowledgments

Thanks to Warren, Kathy, Greg, Andrew, Brian, Linda, Lauren, David, Murray, Carol, Barry, Natalie, Flo, Elsie, Hector, Keeley, Susan, Karen, Gert, Phil, Edna, Jill and Brian, Brianna, Phillip, Paddy and Paul, Stevie, Cary, Rudy and Maggie, Win, Carol M., Vito and Sherry, Elizabeth, and of course, Terry, Nancy, Lion, and Margaret.

Chapter One

It was cold for northern Florida. But it wasn't the temperature, the ocean's stillness or the dead morning air that shrouded the shipyard with a foreboding pall. Abram Harwood knew exactly what it was.

He hurried inside the slipway's observation shack, pushing through co-workers and stretching to see over their heads. Though the shadow of the massive cruise ship darkened the tiny room, it was obvious who'd taken control of the impending launch—Bruce Janus, the ship's young owner. He stood at the window, front and center. The yard's deputy foreman, Joe Price, was at his side.

Price held his walkie-talkie at the ready.

"Wait!" Abram yelled. He was overstepping his bounds, but as the supervisor of the crew who had welded the ship together, he had to do something. He grabbed Price's shoulder and bristled at the impatient look he got in return.

Price shook him off. "I told you," he said, glancing at Janus. "It's not your call."

Janus smiled, his cocky air irritating Abram more than he wanted to admit.

"Wait for Tellemann," Abram said. "He's the one who needs to give the okay."

Janus shook his head. "The weather's perfect. We're launching without him."

A loud voice crackled in Price's walkie-talkie. Someone from the slipway outside. "All set, sir."

Price didn't hesitate. "Release triggers."

"Triggers released," came the response, and the largest liner they'd ever built began moving down the slipway for her first taste of the sea.

No ceremony. No christening for luck. And no Blake Tellemann, the yard superintendent, a man with more launch experience than Price and his crew put together—a man who'd confided in Abram over drinks last night that he feared the ship's launch was doomed, destined to fail. Sure, they'd joked about it. Abram had called Blake an old man in a young man's world. Blake had countered, kidding Abram about being black in a white man's world. But Blake's fear was unmistakable. It's all up to God, he'd said. Once the steel restraints are cut, and the vessel starts to slide down the launching ways, then it's all up to God.

The observation room was silent as the ship headed for the ocean.

Her rudder broke the water's surface.

Propellers next.

There was a hesitation. It was barely perceptible yet serious trouble nonetheless.

"Oh shit." Abram elbowed his way closer to the window, bumping into Bruce Janus and knocking the young man into his chair.

"What? What's going on?" Janus demanded, back on his feet.

"She's binding. Losing momentum," Abram said.

"Son of a bitch, he's right." Price clutched his walkie-talkie. "The ram!" he yelled into the microphone. "Push her with the ram."

The reply was immediate. "She's too damn heavy. You know that."

"Then throw more grease on the ways."

"It won't help. God almighty, Harwood was right. We never should've launched without Blake Tellemann."

Abram could've predicted Armageddon for all it mattered now. He snatched up a spare walkie-talkie and called for Blake, desperate to hear the yard superintendent. But outside the shack, the squeal of metal on wood rose above the shouts of the launching crew. The only voice Abram could hear was Price's as he turned his back to the ship and yelled, "Someone find Tellemann quick. If that tub gets stuck in the launching ways, we're as good as dead."

Janus seized Abram's arm. "Damn it, Harwood, what's happening to my ship?"

Abram pulled away. "Just pray we get her out before the tide falls." Abram grabbed a hard hat and caught the door as several men poured out ahead of him. The screeching sound of more than twenty thousand tons of steel struggling down the launching timbers flooded the tiny observation room.

Hands over his ears, Abram rushed up the five-degree incline of the slipway's floor. A panicked launch crew hurriedly loosened the drag chains. Blake wasn't among them.

Abram jumped into the construction elevator. Within seconds, he was on the highest platform of the gantry, a catwalk level with the ship's top deck. He ran toward the end, to the hundred or more off-duty workers who'd gathered to see the launch. They were shouting, raising their fists, and spurring the ship on. He called for Blake. No response.

Abram scanned the yard beyond the gantry. There was nobody gathered beyond the gate except the spectators and die-hard protesters. "Jesus," he said.

Where the hell was Blake Tellemann? No one had seen him since he'd signed in this morning. Blake had to be here somewhere. If the ship stopped with her aft section in the water—her bow still lodged in the slipway—the stern would be unsupported when the tide fell. A liner could split in two under that kind of stress.

"Jesus," Abram repeated. He turned on his heels, once more checking for movement in the yards, squinting to focus on the fitting-out berth beyond the gantry. Wiping cold sweat from his brow, he came face-to-face with the laboring ship once again.

She was an ugly maiden with no smokestacks and no color on her deckhouses. Once they towed her to her fitting-out berth, they'd transform her into the world's most unique passenger liner. Right now, she was little more than a steel shell with temporary stairs and exposed metal girders.

He narrowed his eyes. *Maybe Blake boarded her to check the auxiliary power supply to the bilge pumps or to prepare the anchor chains himself,* he thought.

Fresh adrenaline shot through Abram's body. He had to get on board. Blake might be trapped inside.

Abram stepped back from the vessel. He was eight decks above her keel. A fifty-foot well deck, both fore and aft, allowed access to the top deck. With her stern now in the water, only the forward well deck was within reach.

Abram unhooked a section of the gantry's safety rail and tossed it away. He gave himself enough distance to get a running start and prayed his momentum would carry him across the six-foot gap between the platform and the ship. He was a tall man, with strong legs that had served him well as a college fullback. But he was twenty years older now. If he tripped or miscalculated his stride, he would fall into the cavity shadowed by the hull, a seventy-foot drop to the slipway's concrete floor below.

He took a long breath and was about to exhale when movement to his left caught his eye.

"Blake?"

Abram focused on the platform beyond the bow. This part of the gantry was temporary, erected to accommodate the ship's excessive length. It had been partially dismantled and roped off before the launch.

At a spot without safety rails, at least two hundred feet away, three men stood calmly near the edge of the catwalk, inches from the deadly drop.

Abram yelled at them.

With the ongoing scream of the ship, the threesome didn't hear him.

He decided to run within shouting distance then continue his search for Blake.

Abram took a step, but the off-duty workers nearly threw him from his feet as they rushed past him, toward the elevators. They didn't slow to sidestep Abram. Nor did they seem to notice the three men in their dangerous location.

Using quick, short strides, Abram moved at an angle through the workmen, finally reaching the safety rail several yards forward. As the workers brushed past, he braced himself and took a deep breath, cupping his hands to his mouth. "You there, make way. Get back, for Christ's sake."

None of the threesome moved.

Abram shouted again, but the words caught in his throat as someone crashed into him, throwing him off balance. He doubled over the safety rail, his hard hat falling from his head. The hat bounced several times before coming to rest on the concrete below.

Using the metal barrier for support, Abram hustled down the catwalk and waved. "You're too close! You got to get out of there!" he yelled.

They turned, but did not move. Abram's hands tightened into fists. *Who let these guys into the yard and what are they trying to prove?* Their clothes looked like costumes. One wore an old-fashioned naval uniform. The other two were dressed in dated business suits, the shorter guy carrying a fancy cane and the tallest holding his jacket over his shoulder, his shirtsleeves rolled up.

Before Abram could speak or take another step, the pitch of the ship's cry changed to a nightmarish sound, then died away as the great liner stopped.

Abram glanced down the length of the hull toward the ocean. Tugs, ready to escort the ship to her berth, jostled near the stern, unsure what to do.

It was a shipbuilder's worst nightmare. Only half of the ship had made it to the water. And the yard's most qualified man was missing.

Abram again turned to face the costumed men, but they were gone. *They might have slipped past me while I was surveying the ship, but I doubt it.* He checked the gantry. No one. He feared the worst.

He crossed the barricade quickly and cautiously and walked into the restricted area. He stopped at the edge of the catwalk where the three men had been. Abram felt he could reach out and touch the hull's cold wall. Yet he realized the gap was closer to ten feet than three.

Carefully, he bent over and grabbed the edge of the platform. The contrast between the looming darkness of the hull and the brightness of the morning blurred his vision, making him question what was real and what was not. He felt dizzy and shut his eyes for a moment, then forced himself to focus on the slipway below.

He swallowed hard. "My God."

The ship's huge starboard anchor had paid out to its bitter end. Blake was on the bottom of the slipway, trapped under the three-foot links of the anchor's deadly chain.

Chapter Two

A minute seemed like a hundred years. Finally, the construction elevator reached the bottom. Abram bolted through the doors, racing up the slipway floor toward the ship's fallen anchor. "Get it off him!" he shouted. "Hurry, let's move!"

Abram felt someone grab his arm. He twisted away. "Pull up the chain. Get a lift out here."

Someone else tried to stop Abram, but he barely slowed. "At the bow," he yelled. "Tellemann is down."

"Harwood. Stay back." It was Price's voice.

Abram ran harder. He didn't see Price until the deputy foreman darted in front of him, blocked him, and nearly tackled him.

"Blake," Abram called, trying to shove Price aside.

Two dockworkers took Abram's arms. Price grabbed his shoulders and said, "There's nothing you can do." Abram shook his head, but Price's grip was solid. "Listen to me. You can't help Tellemann," he said, his face close enough to feel his heavy breath.

But Abram could see past him. He could see the bow, the anchor, and the figure trapped by the heavy links.

Price followed his stare. "I've sent a crew to winch up the anchor and get him out of there. We need to get this ship out."

Abram fought a sickening feeling that rose from his stomach and swelled at the base of his throat. "To hell with the ship."

"No," Price said. "Blake would want to see it sail."

Abram tried once more to pull himself from the grip of his co-workers, but there was no point. *They're right. I can't help Blake now.* He swallowed hard. "Damn it. What was Blake doing down there?"

"I don't know," Price said. "I doubt we'll ever know."

Abram focused on Price. "You're responsible for this."

He stiffened. "It was an accident."

"The anchor chains should've been secured."

"They were, Abram. The windlasses were checked before the launch."

He studied Price for a moment before activity near the bow caught his attention. The medics had arrived, and several crewmen were standing by. Three men stood calmly to the side, the same three who'd been on the platform. As Abram watched, they drifted into the middle of the activity, or perhaps it encompassed them. Either way, all three disappeared, their curious presence overshadowed by the tragic loss of a good and trusted man. Abram's voice wavered. "Did anybody see it happen?"

"Not that I know of." Price eased his hands from Abram's shoulders.

"Somebody needs to call his wife."

Price nodded.

Abram glanced at the ship. Like a massive headstone, the steel hull towered above, motionless.

Still working at the ship's side, the launching crew yelled to one another as they poured more grease on the ways. Perhaps they didn't realize their yard superintendent was at the bow. Or perhaps Blake's death fueled their determination to save the ship, to see her sail, a tribute to the many years he'd dedicated to their trade.

Abram watched as more men gathered around, dragging in portable generators now, connecting welding gear, and firing up torches.

Abram looked straight at Price when he realized what was going on. "You idiot. The weather wasn't perfect. It was too cold. The grease stiffened up."

"Maybe. I don't know. We're heating it up just in case."

Abram braced himself. He wanted to hit Price, plant a hard punch to the jaw. "You son of a bitch! You should've waited for Blake and told Janus to go screw himself!"

Price didn't shrink away, nor did he raise a hand in defense. *I should drop this asshole to the concrete. Nobody's stopping me*, Abram thought. Instead, he relaxed his hand and turned to the ship. There was a low, reverberating groan.

"Look out! There she goes!" someone yelled.

She was moving again, ever so slightly, but gaining momentum nonetheless.

Abram checked the bow. An ambulance crew had moved Blake to a gurney, a sheet covering his body. They were wheeling him away.

"I know he was your friend," Price said. "I'm sorry."

* * * *

Three days later, more than two hundred people gathered at a quiet seaside cemetery to lay Blake Jakob Tellemann to rest.

Abram and the other pallbearers carried the casket. He stood beside Tracy, Blake's wife. "How are you holding up?" he asked.

She wiped her cheek, glancing at her twin teenage daughters, Maddie and Mack. "It's Maddie I'm worried about," she said. "She's barely said a word."

Abram swallowed hard, struggling with a knot in his throat. "I'd give anything for this to be different."

She nodded, taking his hand.

Reverend Scott spoke of ashes and dust, the words sounding empty and mundane in reference to a man who'd given so much and had so much left to give. Abram scanned the mourners. He was proud of the turnout from the yard. Many industry dignitaries were also in attendance, including Janus, though he kept his head down and stood at the fringe of the crowd. Beyond them, the ocean blended with a blue sky. Abram could smell orange blossoms, their scent carried by a light breeze that rattled the leaves of the live oak trees. Overhead, a seagull circled and squawked. It tried to land under the pines at the road but was scared away when two police cruisers came racing up. Abram wondered if they were there to direct traffic after the service, though it seemed unnecessary for such a secluded area.

Reverend Scott finished a passage from the Bible and closed the book, holding it to his chest. He looked over the crowd, his eyes pausing on Maddie. "It's hard to let him go," he said. "But remember, Blake was a man who believed that everything happens for a reason. He had faith in the wisdom of a greater power." Raising his hand and closing his eyes, he said, "I pray you find peace."

He then motioned to Tracy, Maddie, and Mack, and they each placed a rose on Blake's casket as it was lowered into the ground. Abram escorted them back to their car.

"He's right, you know," Tracy said before getting in.

He hugged her, not knowing what to say.

In his truck, he joined the procession exiting the cemetery. He saw four officers at the side of the road struggling to keep a group of fifty people at bay.

Protestors? At a funeral?

"It's a warning," someone from the group shouted.

Another yelled, "Don't let it take anyone else."

Abram squinted to see some of the placards. "Let the past rest in peace," whatever that meant, was scribbled on one. Another one, which would've been amusing under different circumstances, showed Janus with devil horns.

As the procession picked up speed, a tall man in a cassock broke from the crowd. He ran down the length of the cars, offering a flyer to each driver. Before Abram could get his window up, the man tossed one into the truck.

Between glances at the road, Abram read the piece of paper. He shook his head.

Centered on the page, in large, bold letters, was the message:

Have we not learned?
Will not the past come back to haunt us?
Honor their sacrifice.
Destroy the Titan.

Chapter Three

"*Titan's Sister?*" Abram's father, Clay Harwood, asked. "That's what they're gonna call her?"

Abram threw back his face shield. "Yep."

He killed the gas to his welding torch and stood to admire the framing he'd built for a promenade door. But his eyes were drawn to the ship a hundred feet away, moored to the dock where he was working.

During her launch ten months ago, she'd nearly ended her short life broken in two, an unsalvageable wreck, just like *Titanic*, the ship she was modeled after. Despite that fearful start, she floated formidably in the water and was now nearly fitted and ready to sail. Abram often thought of Blake when he looked at her.

The investigators had ruled his death an accident. They didn't point to any specific factor. Rather, a freakish culmination of events was to blame.

They said Blake had been on the ship, probably checking the chain stopper on the forecastle deck, when he tripped, hit his head, and fell unconscious. Price's crew might've noticed him if they'd checked that area, but no one thought it was necessary. In the unlikely event that the anchor let go during the stress of the launch, the windlass, the machine used to raise or lower the anchor, was supposed to hold. It didn't. Oil had leaked inside the gearing mechanism during an on-site repair, as the windlass was defective from the factory. When the chain started to pay out, one of the stopper cables snared Blake and pulled him to his death, they said. A tragedy. No one to blame.

Abram found it difficult to grasp. Random events had come together at just the right time and just the right place to seal Blake's fate. *It's like the universe conspired against him. If only I had gotten there sooner, I could've pulled him to safety.*

ABram hadn't forgotten about the costumed men who'd distracted him that day. *They better hope they never cross my path again...*

"*Titan's Sister*," his father repeated, pulling Abram's thoughts back to the present.

Taking off his welder's helmet, Abram again studied the imposing ship stretching in front of them. "Yeah," he said. "A twin sister."

"Kinda stupid, if you ask me."

"That's what the owner wanted."

Clay shook his head. "There's a lot in a name, son."

Abram knew that was true. As he looked at the sleek, black hull, the four yellow and black funnels rising amidships, and the 150-foot masts both fore and aft, Abram wondered why this vessel wasn't simply called *Titanic*. She looked exactly like the historic liner, just as Algo Cruise Lines had specified. She was set to sail in mid-April, less than a month away.

Abram checked the valves on his cutting torch and hung his helmet over the equipment. "They want a full two weeks for sea trials then some time to work out any bugs. It puts my men under the gun to frame the windows and enclose the promenade."

"You'll do fine," Clay said.

Abram wasn't so sure. As the ship's maiden voyage drew near, the number of onlookers beyond the shipyard's fence had steadily increased. Most were just curious. But the small God-fearing group who'd demonstrated at Blake's funeral had gathered as well. Their numbers growing each day, they'd even set up something of a camp, their grim faces and crudely painted placards solemnly denouncing the resurrection of this ship. Security guards were ever-present, and occasionally, Abram spotted a white Ford Crown Victoria parked outside Klipper's gates. Two occupants were always visible behind the tinted windows. He suspected it was the police, keeping an eye on things.

Clay took a few steps from the ship but didn't entirely turn his back on it. He removed his cap and scratched his head, squinting as he assessed the vessel. "It's pretty big."

"Yep, a sixth of a mile long. And from her keel to the top of her funnels, nearly as high as a sixteen story apartment building."

"Almost larger than life," Clay said.

Abram picked up a rag and wiped his hands. "She does seem alive somehow." Elegant, almost boastful, he thought, with thousands of eyes winking at him as the sparkling ocean was reflected in the rows of portholes that spanned the length of the ship.

"Come on," Clay said. "Let's get out of here. That thing's giving me the creeps."

Abram smiled and stretched the kinks out of his back. He checked his watch. "Okay, Pop, where's lunch?"

"Where else?" Clay said, starting down the dock. "The Ocean Shanty. And I'm buying."

Abram's smile widened to a grin. The last time Pop was in town they'd spent several hours in the Shanty, taking advantage of the all-you-can-eat cod special and indulging in a pitcher of dark beer, Pop's favorite. They'd discussed everything from the best way to make a fillet weld to the women currently drifting through their lives.

With a few quick steps, Abram caught up to his father. "So, what's the occasion anyway? What brings you into town?"

"Just wanted to see you, son. Thought I might stay over for a few days."

Abram slowed his pace to allow for his father's aging knees. The sun appeared from behind a cloud.

They reached the gate, and the security guard buzzed them through. It was quiet today. A few people stood at the fence, some kicking dirt and waiting for something to happen, others poking their camera lenses through its interwoven spines, hoping to get an unobstructed shot of the ship. None bothered Abram or Clay as they headed to the parking lot.

"You're welcome to stay at the condo," Abram offered when they reached his truck. "But I'm not sure how much spare time I'll have."

"That's fine. I can amuse myself. But tell you what. Make it up to me by promising we'll take off somewhere when you're done. I know some great places in the Keys."

Abram laughed as they got in his truck. "I know you do, Pop, but I've got a surprise—two first-class tickets for the *Sister*'s maiden voyage."

"No way. I'm not going. Period," Clay said.

Abram waited until they had to stop for a red light at the corner before asking, "Why not?"

"Light's green," his father said.

Abram shifted gears and turned his attention back to the street. "She's state of the art—the most advanced ship conceived."

"Isn't that what they said about *Titanic*? A lot of people drowned."

Abram slipped his Chevy into second then third without comment.

Clay said, "This is about Blake isn't it?"

"What?" Abram tightened his grip on the steering wheel.

"You figure you owe him something. That taking a chance on this ship will somehow set things straight."

"Taking a chance?" Abram hit the brakes to avoid the car in front of him.

Clay tugged at his seat belt. "What's this ship all about anyway?" he asked. "I hear that owner guy, Janus, is nuts, better off making tea cozies in a loony bin than building any kind of a ship."

"The *Sister*'s a gimmick, okay?" Abram said, getting the truck back up to speed. "To attract a younger crowd."

"Because the *older* crowd is too smart."

"You're not smart," Abram said. "You're superstitious."

"Call it what you want. You don't risk what few years you got left by tempting fate."

Abram was traveling too fast but what the hell. "Odds were a million to one," he said, "that *Titanic* sank in the first place."

"That's what you said about Blake's death."

"Pop, please."

"I've toured the *Queen Mary*. That's enough for me."

"This ship's different."

Clay turned quickly to look at his son. "No. We never learn. Pride comes before a fall. Like your grandfather, rest his soul, thinking he didn't need a life jacket in a rowboat. Let some other fools go. Not us."

Abram signaled and pulled into the curb lane behind a bus. The restaurant was just ahead on the right. Before the entrance, the bus slowed and stopped, leaving Abram to wait while passengers loaded and unloaded. He eased his grip on the steering wheel and rolled his shoulders to stretch out the tension. In the calmest voice he could muster, he said, "I'm going, Pop. That's the end of it."

* * * *

The Ocean Shanty provided a great view of the curving coastline, and Klipper Shipyards was visible in the distance. Because the place was crowded, a table in the center of the dining room was all the hostess could offer. They ordered beer, catfish, and fries. Halfway through their meal, the waitress wandered by. She was about to ask Abram and Clay how lunch was coming along, when a large man at a window table interrupted her. "Look! Jesus, look!" He pointed at something past the shoreline.

The waitress rolled her eyes, suggesting that he'd had one too many beers. When she started to speak, a chorus of shouts cut her off. Everyone was looking in the direction of the shipyard.

Abram jumped to his feet and rushed to the window.

The dock—the very spot where Abram and Clay had stood looking at *Titan's Sister* only half an hour ago—was totally engulfed in flames.

Chapter Four

Sirens rose and fell in the distance, and fire engines screamed through Klipper's gates. The blaze swept down the *Sister*'s fitting-out berth, buildings and tents exploding and cranes and supplies disappearing in the black smoke. Abram spun his truck to a stop and jumped out as the first wave of fire engines charged in. Rescue squads and command vehicles raced into position. In the distance, the sirens of another alarm blared.

The air was acrid, full of suspended ash and laden with fumes from the growing fire. With frantic gestures, the commanding officer directed his fire crew into position. A truck screeched to a stop in front of Abram. Men hustled from the vehicle and pulled out hoses. The driver, barely taking time to set the emergency brake, bolted from the cab to start the pumps and check the pressure gauges. The flames snapped with energy, transparent from the heat one moment, then glowing an angry red the next.

The heat stung Abram's face. The fire thundered continuously. It took him a minute to comprehend what he was seeing within the bedlam. At first, it seemed impossible. Abram could see the ship through the chaos, and against the backdrop of its dark hull was the outline of a person staggering in the heat.

"Pop, look!"

Clay was breathing hard. "Stay out of the way, son."

Abram looked for help. "Wait here," he said.

Jumping through the tangle of hoses, Abram played a dangerous game of hopscotch to reach the closest firefighter. The man struggled to steady one of the large lines while another two firefighters fought to direct its heavy spray.

"There's a man in there," Abram hollered.

"What?"

Abram pointed frantically toward the ship.

Grappling with the line as his partners pushed forward, the firefighter nearly lost his grip. He shook his head. "I don't see anyone. Get back. Get out of the way!"

Abram hurried closer. He found the battalion chief. Yelling the same message, Abram pointed in the direction of the ship. Immediately, the chief put his portable radio to his mouth. Poised to shout new orders, he studied the fire intently, but even Abram, knowing precisely where to look, couldn't see the man anymore.

"He was right there," Abram shouted.

The chief shook his head. "Couldn't have been."

More holes appeared in the fire now, places where the blaze had consumed the structures on the concrete dock so completely there was nothing left to burn. Water from the hoses pushed the flames back.

Checking around, Abram spotted a rescue truck, the door to the side compartment open. Hanging inside was a yellow, Nomex jacket. On the bumper sat a helmet. He hustled to the truck, slipped into the heat-resistant gear, and turned to face the fire once more. Tightening the strap of the helmet under his chin, Abram decided it was now or never. Someone had to help the guy trapped near the ship.

Abram took several short pulls of air before filling his lungs. Holding his breath, he raced into a tunnel-sized gap in the flames.

He moved quickly, hunched over, his arms in front of his head to protect his face. Small clumps of flames danced on the blackened concrete. The ship was right in front of him. But he couldn't see anyone.

Abram took a few more determined steps. His pulse quickened as his body begged for fresh air.

There was time for one last desperate look. He could see nothing. Not even the ship's hull to get his bearing.

Just turn around, he told himself. But behind him, the smoke had grown thicker and darker. The tunnel was collapsing.

The smoke now circled him. With it came the heat. And the flames, no longer visible through a cloak of flying ashes, snapped from all directions.

Abram wrapped his arms around his chest, his lungs pleading for oxygen. He ran in a direction that he could only guess was toward safety.

He tripped and staggered, but managed to stay on his feet. Steadying himself, Abram looked over his shoulder. He'd tripped over a corpse, the face black and blistered, smoldering clothes fused to a contorted body.

Abram closed his eyes. He could barely breathe, the lack of oxygen finally knocking him to his knees. He tried to yell for help but his voice stuck in his throat.

"Oh, God," he cried, praying his drained body would persevere.

Abram began to crawl.

Eventually, Abram heard a soft, recurring voice and felt a cool breath on his skin. Saints. Angels. Heaven. But an earthly heaven, filled with the sound of lapping waves and a scent of fresh air blowing lazily from the ocean.

Thank God. He was safely at the end of the *Sister*'s fitting-out berth. Abram pulled hard for oxygen. At first, his lungs barely moved. Eventually, they responded, grasping for the unadulterated air, forcing him to cough until he'd purged them of the sickening smoke. He tossed his helmet away and lay on the dock, grateful for the cool concrete underneath.

After a minute or two, Abram staggered to his feet, every muscle in his body aching. Cleansing tears streamed down his cheeks. With no strength for anything else, he wiped his face and looked around.

On both sides and in front of him, the light-blue ocean softly rippled. This section of the dock stretched into the water, well beyond the length of the *Sister*. Because it was clear of vehicles and structures, it wasn't within reach of the fire.

And he had company. Someone else had escaped, apparently unscathed. Abram squinted to be sure. At the edge of the dock, sitting with his back against a post, was a slight yet authoritative-looking man. He was dressed in an old-style suit with narrow pants and a neatly tailored coat with tails. At his side was a cane, though it was too elaborate to have any functional value.

Abram moved closer. "It's you, you son of a bitch!"

The man didn't move. His eyes were closed, his head lowered, as if he were unconscious.

* * * *

Shit. Crouching beside the man, Abram shook him lightly. "You okay?" *He doesn't look dead, but his face is too white.* Abram stood, tugged off his firefighter's jacket and tossed it aside. He was bending over to cover the man's upper body when the man's eyes popped open. Abram jumped back, landing on his butt. "Son of a …! You scared me, man."

No response. *Either he doesn't give a shit, or he can't talk.*

"What's with you, huh?"

The man's eyes shifted. Abram got to his feet and considered what to do. He wasn't in great shape either. His hands were throbbing. The knees in his pants were gone, shredded by the coarse concrete, and the exposed flesh tingled. Taking in any kind of a heavy breath caused a coughing fit.

Over his shoulder, the fire was contained, but it continued to belch heat and black smoke from the remains of tents and trailers.

Abram turned to the mysterious man. "Listen. We have to wait for help. Just take it easy, okay?"

Abram thought he saw a nod.

"What's your name?"

Nothing.

"Where you from?"

Nothing.

Damn it, who is this guy? Crossing his arms, Abram sat against a mooring post. He considered searching the man's suit pockets for identification but then thought better of it. The outfit indicated the man was someone of means, and a black man searching through a skinny white guy's clothes would undoubtedly be misconstrued.

"How be I call you Spin?" Abram said. "Short for spindly."

That didn't get a rise out of him.

Abram picked up his Nomex jacket and turned his attention back to the dwindling fire.

He heard shouts. He listened for voices until he could see a group of firefighters through the lingering smoke. They'd closed in on a charred heap near the middle of the dock. Abram wasn't sure, but he thought that heap used to be his welding tent. He tried to yell, but his voice was still raspy. He eventually got their attention by waving his jacket.

Four firefighters dropped their hoses and came running to the end of the dock, two from the group near his tent and two others who'd been dousing hot spots in the wreckage with blasts of high-pressure water.

The man didn't seem to care. He was focused on the hull of the ship, his lips moving.

Abram knelt. "What'd you say?"

The words were barely a whisper, if they were that at all.

"Say again." Abram bent his ear close to the man's lips.

"Forty-one, twenty-seven, fifty, and zero-eight."

"What about them?"

Before the guy could answer, the firemen were on top of them. The rescuers had fire blankets, and they swung one around Abram to protect his face and body. He couldn't see anything except the grey fiberglass fabric in front of his eyes. He heard the rising sound of an ambulance, though, racing to help the man in shock.

But it was Abram who was dropped onto a gurney and lifted inside the responding rescue vehicle. Its siren rang in his ears as a paramedic placed an oxygen mask over Abram's nose and mouth and started an intravenous line. He heard the back door slam. Someone banged on it, telling the driver it was time to move out.

Abram looked around. An attendant was at his side. No one else. *What the heck happened to Spin?*

*   *   *   *

"Pop, is that you?" Abram needed a moment to focus. He'd been knocked out by sedatives but heard arguing, loud voices in his hospital room.

"I've already told them to leave," Clay said.

"Told who?" Abram rubbed his eyes with his forearm. Except for a dull overhead lamp and the late afternoon light from the window, the room was dark. On the window side of his bed was his father. On the other side was a man wearing a jacket and tie. A woman stood at the footboard.

"Mr. Harwood," the man said. "I'm Detective Morgan." He motioned to the woman. "This is my partner, Detective Jones."

"They want to know about the fire," Clay said. "I already told them we were at lunch."

"We just have a few questions."

"Son, you need your rest."

"I'm okay." Abram pulled off his oxygen mask.

"You're very lucky," Morgan said.

"Yeah." The doctor had already explained that he hadn't sustained any serious burns in the fire, but they'd bandaged his hands and knees because of blisters and scrapes. Once an hour, a nurse squirted saline in his eyes to cleanse them.

Morgan pulled up a chair and sat. "Why'd you run into the fire, Mr. Harwood?"

Abram tried to suppress a cough with no luck.

"Need some water?"

Abram nodded. Morgan picked up a plastic glass, and Abram took two sips through the straw then leaned back on his pillow. "I thought someone needed help."

Morgan made a note in his book. "Why didn't you leave that to the firefighters?"

"At one point I could see him so clearly. I thought I could run in and get back out without any problem."

"But you couldn't find him," Morgan stated.

"No. He wasn't the guy at the end of the dock, I'm pretty sure."

The female detective spoke. "What guy?" she asked. From what Abram could tell in the murkiness of his room, Detective Jones was tall, had light brown skin, and was tougher than Morgan.

Abram said, "When my eyes cleared after crawling through the smoke, I saw this guy. He was dressed weird. In an old-fashioned suit."

Morgan scratched something else down. "What happened to him?"

"Don't know. I didn't see him after the rescue. He wasn't burned or anything. I think he was in shock."

Morgan tapped his pencil on his chin. He had a wrinkled face and suit to match. "You're sure of this?" he asked.

"Yes, of course. Why?"

"Well, it's interesting, Mr. Harwood," Morgan said. "The paramedics treated only one man. Yourself."

"That's ridiculous."

"They wouldn't have any reason to lie."

"They must be mistaken."

"I'm afraid not."

Abram closed his eyes tightly. When he reopened them, he looked directly at Morgan and swallowed hard. "What about the corpse?"

"Corpse?"

"Yes, in the fire."

"We didn't find any remains, Mr. Harwood." The detective stood. "I think you'd better start giving us the straight story here."

Clay clutched the bed rail. "Son, tell them to go away."

"I don't understand," Abram persisted.

Morgan closed his notebook and slipped it into his suit pocket. "Well, let me try to explain." He crossed his arms and leaned backward, balancing on his heels. "Witnesses say they saw a small explosion close to the center of the dock seconds before the fire erupted. As I understand it, that's where your welding tent is ... was."

Abram's voice stuck in his throat. *An explosion at my welding tent?*

"And," Morgan said, "we found one of your propane tanks with the valve left open. Why propane, Mr. Harwood?"

Clay pushed past the female detective. "What the hell are you getting at? I saw Abram secure his equipment myself."

"Calm down, sir." Morgan put a hand on Clay's shoulder. "Our questions are just standard police procedure."

Clay knocked Morgan's arm away. "Sounds more like an accusation to me."

"Of course not, Mr. Harwood."

Abram was lost for words.

Pop turned to Detective Jones.

She held her arms tightly against her chest, her feet spread. Clay hardened his own features, standing as defiantly as the two detectives.

She said, "I think we'd better give this man some rest."

"You shouldn't have woken him in the first place," Clay responded.

Detective Jones held the door open. Morgan turned before they left and addressed Clay. "She was talking about you, Mr. Harwood," Morgan said. "You're the one who needs the rest."

Chapter Five

The morning was bleak and uninviting, but Abram didn't mind. He'd spent two days in the hospital, forty-eight hours longer than he thought necessary, and he was happy to be outside, regardless of how dismally the day expressed itself.

Relishing the air's clean scent after last night's rain, he walked several blocks, pulling in long breaths and filling his lungs completely. He picked up the *Sentinel* at a newspaper stand and hailed a cab for home.

When he arrived, his father had a late breakfast waiting: bacon and eggs, sausage, grits, biscuits with gravy, and steaming hot coffee.

He sat down eagerly to Pop's home-cooked meal, eating more than his share of his father's Cajun eggs.

"So," Clay said, wiping his chin. "Did you hear any more from those detectives?"

Abram pushed his plate aside. "No, not since you were there."

"That Morgan guy, I'd like to—"

"I know, Pop," Abram said. "But we've got to let it go." He picked up his newspaper. "You want sports or fashion?"

"Very funny." Clay snapped up the sports section.

Abram settled back with the local news. "Looks like the *Sister* is still making headlines. Hard to tell from the picture how bad she's burned."

"I know." Clay's voice came from behind the paper. "They didn't release a lot of details."

Abram skimmed the article until he found what he was looking for. "Says here only one person injured. Treated and released."

"That'd be you."

"And no fatalities."

"Nope." Clay flipped to a new page. "Damn it. The Marlins lost again. Thirteen to two."

"Strange," Abram said, still focused on the page.

"Not when you consider the rubber arms in their bull pen." Clay folded the paper and tossed it on the table. "Still, losing by eleven is kind of embarrassing."

Abram looked at his father absently for a second. Finally, Abram said, "Say, Pop. Do the numbers forty-one, twenty-seven, fifty, and zero-eight ring any bells?"

Clay shrugged. "Not really, unless—"

"What?"

Clay leaned forward, picking up his spoon and shaking it at Abram. "Now, I'm not a gambling man, but if I were playing bingo with those numbers, I'd be close to filling the G column."

Abram shook his head. "I don't think that's it." He turned his attention back to the article. "Says here the fire marshal has released his preliminary findings."

"This oughta be good." Clay sat back and folded his arms.

"Although the cause remains undetermined," Abram read, "there's no indication of arson." He sat back as well. "Doesn't explain much, does it?"

"You should highlight it and send a copy to Morgan." Under his breath, he added, "Assuming that fool detective can read."

Abram rubbed his budding beard with the back of his bandaged hand. "I think I should get down to the yard."

Clay didn't respond.

Abram tapped the table and stood. "I want to see what's happening for myself."

Getting up as well, Clay caught Abram's eyes. He held them with a don't-be-a-fool look that Abram knew well. "Listen to me, Abram," Clay said. "It's obvious there's something wrong with that ship, and it's taking you down with it."

"That's ridiculous."

"Is it? First your friend Blake. Now this."

Abram closed his eyes, rolled his head back to pull kinks out of his neck, and stretched his shoulders. "Pop," Abram said, mustering a resolute look of his own. "She's not cursed."

For a moment, Abram was sure his father was going to argue, but Clay looked away and his expression softened. "Okay," he said. "But you can't work for a few days, son. Trust your old man. Take a break from it."

Abram rubbed his chin with his arm. "All right," he said. *After I visit the yard.*

* * * *

His father was right about one thing. Abram couldn't do much—including operating the gearshift in his truck—without the full use of his hands. He called for a cab.

A few minutes after ten, the cab pulled to within a block of Klipper's gates. The cabbie was reluctant to get any closer to the crowd lining the shipyard's fence. The group looked harmless to

Abram. Most of the people were jockeying for a good view of the fire's aftermath. Even the diehard protesters seemed more interested in the activities inside the shipyard than in making a statement to passers-by.

Abram paid the driver and pushed his way through the crowd to the security guard.

"What's going on?" Abram asked over loud cheers and boos.

"They just started hosing her down," the guard said. He held out his hand. "Clearance card, please."

"Huh?" The guard had been at Klipper so long that everyone considered him a fixture in the booth. He knew Abram well and normally waved him through without checking ID.

"Rules," the guard said. "Nothing personal."

"Right." Abram fished his card out of his wallet.

With long, labored strokes, the guard printed Abram's name and time of entry in the spiral bound logbook and then let him pass.

A damp, festering stench greeted Abram as he rounded the corner to the fitting-out berth. He knew that nothing on the dock would be salvageable. Still, he was surprised by the eerie nature of what little remained.

Heaps of ashes and twisted metal littered the blackened concrete like memorials for the tents, trailers, and supplies that the fire had destroyed. Yellow caution tape, broken in several places, flapped in the subtle breeze, looking as abandoned and desolate as the burned and water-soaked remains it attempted to cordon off.

Abram didn't immediately look at the ship. Rather, he found the ends of the mooring lines on the dock and followed them with his eyes up to the *Sister*.

She was in good shape. The forward section of her starboard hull would have to be repainted, and she'd probably suffered some smoke damage. But her white deckhouses and mustard funnels shone against the grey day. Klipper's men were washing her down.

"Harwood! Over here, damn it."

Abram turned abruptly. Behind him, Floyd Bain, the new yard superintendent, stood at the door of a temporary trailer.

"Harwood, get your black ass in here."

Abram glanced at the ship and then walked toward Bain, pacing himself. After Tellemann's death, the crew had been blessed with a toothpick-chewing, seat-of-the-pants yard superintendent who Abram had never learned to like.

"Christ, man. What're ya doin' in the yard?" Bain asked.

"I wanted to see what happened. Is that a problem?"

The superintendent leaned on the doorframe of the trailer, crossing his arms. "Better be a fast look. Dozers are comin' within the hour, and by late afternoon scrubbers will have this place back in order."

"You can't do that. Not until they figure out what happened."

"The fire marshal says he's got all that he needs. The world doesn't sit on its ass, you know, just 'cause you got sore hands. By the way, am I gonna have to certify a new supervising welder?"

Abram shook his head. Klipper was under the gun, and qualified welders were hard to come by. "No," Abram said. "I'll be back before your supplies are on the dock."

"Good. Now get outta here. Anybody sees you around, there's gonna be questions."

"Why?"

The superintendent spat. "Some of the other guys wonder if your equipment maybe had a little leak."

"That's impossible. You know it."

"Yep, I know it," Bain said, pulling the words from the back of his throat. "Just between you and me, though, I betcha there's a cover-up somewhere. Always is when there's a lot of money around."

"Maybe, but why?"

"The way I hear it, Algo's up to its ass in alligators with this tub. But hell," Bain added, throwing his hands up in the air, "none of my business."

Abram left the trailer, shaking his head. He didn't bother with the courtesy of saying good-bye to the superintendent. Nor did Abram intend to leave the yards right away.

Instead, he traced his path from two days ago as best he could.

As he walked, his boots thudded on the ground, the solid sound of concrete mellowed by the soft coating of ashes. The stench stung his nose. Each step toward the end of the dock heightened his senses, and he could almost feel the heat of the now-dead fire on his face and hands.

With his mind so focused beyond the ravaged berth, on the soft blue ripples of the ocean at the end of the dock, Abram tripped, and when he looked down to see what had been in his path, the image of a fire-eaten corpse flashed through his mind. He quickly looked away, though the charred heap was nothing more than the melted remains of a small tent.

Abram continued down the dock, faster now, until he was clear of the burned area.

He stopped near the place where he had waited for the rescue team. The helmet and jacket he'd worn were still there, neither of them the traditional yellow but scorched black, last night's rain doing little to clean them. He was hoping to find some evidence of Spin being there. His cane, perhaps, or a button or hankie.

After ten minutes of futile searching, Abram turned to the ocean. Its familiar scent filled his nostrils, and he could taste the salt in the air. The water was calm, peaceful.

He sat on one of the dock's bollards.

How could the firefighters not remember saving Spin? he thought. *And the corpse? If that was just the remains of a tent, I guess I might have imagined the guy at the end of the dock, too.*

Abram nodded, watching the rise and fall of the ocean's unbroken surface. *Pop is right. I need some time off, even if it's just a few hours at the park to cheer for the floundering Marlins.*

Chapter Six

His father was out when Abram reached home. In the kitchen, he washed down two painkillers and noticed the light flashing on the answering machine.

Morgan's partner, the woman detective, had left a message for him to phone the South Gable's third precinct. Odd, Abram thought, that she'd be placing a call to him. By all accounts, the police investigation was over.

Abram scratched down her number and headed for the living room to return the call.

Detective Jones wasn't in. Nor was Morgan. Abram left a message. He put his feet up and rested his head on a pillow so he could see out the sliding glass door. His condo was on the beach, ground level, facing the ocean. Abram watched vacationers running in and out of the water, some holding hands with their friends, others towing rubber rafts or surfboards.

It wasn't long before the painkillers took hold, and soon he closed his eyes with a promise of sleep not far off. His mind drifted back to the ship, to the work yet to be done after she was cleaned up. He dozed until a knock at the door awoke him.

He wearily got to his feet. "Who is it?"

"Detective Jones," came the response. "I got a message you'd called."

Abram looked through the peephole. *My God, she's beautiful.* He fumbled with the lock, eventually getting the door open.

"Good afternoon, Mr. Harwood." She held out her hand.

Abram hesitated because of the bandages. She noticed and withdrew her hand.

"Mind if I come in?" she asked, but she stepped through the door without waiting for a response.

Abram followed her inside, trying not to stare.

She didn't hide the fact that she was checking him out. "Nice place," she said, surveying the room. "Tidy."

Tidy? "I like it."

Still sizing up his condo, she said, "I happened to be in the neighborhood."

Abram laughed at the cliché. "In the neighborhood?"

"Yes." She turned and looked at him, obviously not amused. "Your father in?"

As attractive as she was, Abram remained cautious. She was Detective Morgan's partner, and Pop had warned him about Morgan. "Look," Abram said. "We told you all we knew."

"Relax, Mr. Harwood. We move quickly and push hard in all our investigations. Anything could be a lead. I'm sure you understand."

"Not really. No doubt my father won't."

"He did seem upset." She glanced at the closed doors leading from the living room. "Does he live with you?"

Abram moved between her and the guest room, stopping short of his own bedroom door. "My dad's staying over for a few days," he said. "Why?"

She shrugged. "Just curious." Her voice remained stiff, although her expression softened slightly. "Here's the thing, Mr. Harwood," she said. "You went running into that inferno with little protection. Civilians see a hero. We see a suspect."

Abram stepped back. "I don't get it."

"Your actions fit a certain profile. Part of the arsonist's thrill is sticking around and helping out."

She's fishing, no doubt about it. "But it wasn't arson," he said.

"We couldn't rule it out. Not until we heard from the fire marshal. Especially when you suggested an accomplice might be at large."

Abram narrowed his eyes. "What accomplice?"

"The man you claimed you saw. We talked to everyone who might've seen him." She shook her head. "No leads."

Abram crossed his arms, tucking his bandaged hands under his elbows. He never thought of Spin as an accomplice. "What does it matter now?"

"Maybe it doesn't." A slight but gentle smile crossed her face, and she held up her hands as if offering a truce.

No ring on any finger. "Good," he said.

A seagull squawked, and Abram followed Jones's gaze as it passed to the window and then to the stacks of books he had arranged on the coffee table.

She cleared her throat. "You got some bottled water or a soda or something? I'm parched."

As much as he wanted her to leave, he also wanted her to stay. "Sure," he said. "I'll see what I have."

In the kitchen, Abram took out two of his better glasses, watching the detective through the service opening. She was facing him but not looking in his direction. As he popped open a can of soda, she bent over the coffee table to pick up a book.

Her blouse fell from her breasts, exposing a tight T-shirt that just covered her nipples. She lingered in that position without attempting to cover up.

"Ah, shit," he said as soda foamed over the can and soaked into his bandages. When the fizz finally settled, he headed back to the living room, drinks on a tray.

The detective was now standing near the TV, hands in her pants pockets, studying a framed black-and-white photograph on the wall.

"Did you take this?" she asked.

Abram set the drinks on the coffee table. "Yes, in Halifax. It's one of three cemeteries where *Titanic*'s victims are buried."

She raised her eyebrows.

"The cemetery's a popular tourist attraction," he said.

"A tourist attraction? Why?"

Abram shrugged. "I don't know. It speaks to you somehow."

She tilted her head. "It's a good picture."

"Thanks," he said. Studying it himself, he moved closer. He was glad he did. The detective was wearing a nice perfume. Abram cleared his throat. "The sun was just coming up," he said, remembering the morning in the cemetery. "It was the long shadows that I wanted to capture. Not ... the gravestones."

"Why bury the victims in Canada?" she asked.

"*Titanic* was bound for New York from England when it hit the iceberg. Halifax was the closest port."

She turned away, flicking her hand, suggesting she'd heard enough.

Abram pointed to the tray of drinks. "I got you a Pepsi. Hope that's okay."

"Yep."

She sat on the edge of the couch, spreading her legs a little bit to get closer to the coffee table. Abram pulled a chair around with his foot.

"A lot of books you've got here," she said, sifting through the twenty or so titles.

Abram sat back, smiling to himself. *She's good. Wonder what she wants.* "Yeah," he said. "I haven't had time to go through them all yet."

"Looks like they're all about *Titanic*."

"Pretty much."

"Some of these books look really old," she commented. "Are you a collector?"

He shook his head. "They belonged to a friend. His wife found them in their basement and gave them to me after he died."

She picked up a newer book and opened the cover, discovering a business card marking a page inside. "Blake Tellemann? He was a friend of yours?"

"Yeah."

"He was the guy killed during the launch," she said.

"Yes."

She sipped her drink. "I heard the owner … what's his name? Janus. I heard Janus pushed for the launch even though this Blake guy went missing."

"Uh-huh. That's what happened."

Leafing through the book, she leaned back, crossing her legs, her pant cuffs rising up and tightening around her toned calf muscles. She had the legs of a runner. "What's Janus's rush?" she asked.

"Symbolic, I think. *Titanic*'s maiden voyage was in April. So he wants his ship to sail in April. It's costing him a fortune in overtime and inefficiencies."

"A lot of people think he's shrewd—in an eccentric kind of way. I just think he's weird."

Abram laughed out loud. "He's a software genius. It comes with the territory."

She smiled, agreeing with him, catching his eyes before turning her attention back to Blake's book.

Abram shifted in his chair, uncomfortable with the lull in conversation.

"I'm curious, Abram," she finally said, closing the book and setting it on her lap. "Why did Tellemann's wife think you'd be interested in these?"

"What do you mean?" he asked.

"Well, *Titanic*'s not really Black history. Maybe European immigrants'. Not ours."

Abram nodded. "It's hard not to get caught up in it."

"Get caught up in what?"

"The tragedy," he said, taking a sip and setting the glass back down. "A long chain of events resulted in *Titanic*'s fatal collision with an iceberg. What if one link in that chain had been broken?"

She ran her fingers down her neck as if reflecting on what he'd said. Long fingers, he noticed. Manicured nails but of a practical length. She took a prolonged look at Abram's cemetery picture. "It's like trying to make sense of a senseless event," she said.

"Exactly," Abram responded, moving to the edge of his chair. He was surprised she understood. Someone who'd never experienced a tragic loss firsthand usually didn't get it. To lose an aged father or mother, well, nature worked that way. But for those who'd buried a child or experienced the premature death of a friend or relative, it was easy to get lost searching for closure with questions that had no answers.

"You gotta wonder, then," she said, as if reading his thoughts. "Why build the *Sister* and dredge up all that stuff?"

He sat back and took a long, thoughtful breath. "I like her. She's sleek, trim. Graceful. Not like these new cruise ships, which are little more than a barge with a hotel on top."

She uncrossed her legs and stood, pulling her shoulders back. "Yeah, they do look top heavy."

No, they're perfect. Trying not to stare, he got to his feet. "You barely touched your soda."

"Actually what I need is a drink of water."

Abram was quick to get to the kitchen and back.

Melika barely had a sip before returning the glass. She dug a business card from her jacket pocket as she walked to the door. "Here's my number."

Abram took the card between his middle and index finger. "Melika. Nice name."

She hesitated. "Call me," she said.

Abram seriously considered it.

"If you think of anything you can add," she said.

He nodded.

She opened the door, and he followed her into the hallway, returning to his condo only after she was out of sight.

With his knees hurting again, he spread out on the couch, enjoying the soft scent of Melika's perfume still lingering in the room. Feeling good about himself, he closed his eyes, though he knew he wouldn't get back to sleep. After a minute, he reached for the book she'd been interested in, *The Great Sea Disaster of the North Atlantic.*

"Hey," he said out loud. "She took it!"

* * * *

Melika tossed her jacket, notebook, and purse on her office desk. It was a mess, as always, the clutter spilling onto Morgan's work area. Like most partners, they found it more efficient to work as a team with their desks pushed together.

Morgan sat up in his creaky office chair. "Where have you been?" he asked.

"Out on a call."

"Seeing who?"

"Abram Harwood."

"Did you get into his apartment?"

"Yep. I used our standard excuse. Apologizing for you." Melika knew that Morgan was used to her giving him a hard time. He'd once called her attempt at humor dry and combative. Whether that was good or bad, she and Morgan clicked the way most partners didn't. Even better than those on TV.

"Find out anything?" he asked.

She shook her head. "Harwood's got a nice condo. Tidy. Too tidy if you ask me."

"That's hardly a crime."

"And it's on the beach with a killer view. I couldn't afford it, but I don't think he's living beyond his means."

"Probably not. Good craftsmen can make six figures at the yard."

"He's smart, too."

Morgan narrowed his eyes and tilted his head, studying her.

"What?" she asked. "Have I grown a second nose or something?"

A grin crossed his face. He leaned forward. "It's a look I've never seen before, that's for sure."

"What are you talking about?"

Morgan sat back. "You like him," he said.

"That's ridiculous."

"Wait till I tell my wife. She'll love this."

Melika rolled her eyes. "Your wife's just like me. She doesn't pay any attention to you either." Melika pushed her jacket and purse aside. "Can we get back to the case now?"

"Sure." Morgan pulled the lid off a paper coffee cup. "Did Harwood say any more about the guy he claimed he saw?"

"He was defensive."

"You think he's hiding something?" He handed her the coffee.

"I'm pretty sure there's something he's not talking about."

"What's his take on Janus?"

"Not much. I gave him plenty of opportunity, but he didn't say anything bad about the guy."

"That in itself is suspicious."

"No kidding." She took a gulp from the cup and looked at it with a disgusted face. "It's cold." She set it aside. "So what do we got?"

"Apart from the fact that both the Tellemann inquiry and the fire investigation were handled in record time, nothing."

"A lot of money running around for some reason. That reminds me: Harwood said Janus is burning bucks like crazy in overtime and inefficiencies. Whatever that means."

"Yeah, I heard about that. Another example of Janus being in a rush." He pointed to her coffee. "You going to finish that?"

"God, no." She handed it to him. "What's this other example?"

Morgan drank half of the coffee without taking a breath. He wiped his mouth with his sleeve and said, "Let me give you a little lesson on shipbuilding."

Melika rolled her eyes. "Oh, jeez, here we go."

"You'll find this interesting," he said. "Trust me."

"I always do, Morgan."

"See, nowadays they put a ship together in blocks, like Lego, each block fitted in the shop with plumbing, electrical, that kind of stuff. But," he said, spreading his hands like a toastmaster, "Janus didn't want to wait for supplies. They built the ship in blocks, all right, but had to fit her the old-fashioned way. Very time consuming."

"That's why the fire was so big," Melika said. "Stuff that should've been in the blocks was still on the fitting-out dock."

"You get a star."

"Thanks."

"The question is," Morgan said, "why the rush?"

Melika paused. "Harwood said it might have something to do with the *Titanic*. It sailed in April, so *Titan's Sister* should, too."

"I don't think so. Too much money running around just to keep a cruise on schedule."

"So now what?"

"We keep watching. Our job is to make sure nothing happens to that ship before it sails. Right now, we're batting zero for two." He pointed at her desk. "Hey, what's that?"

"What?"

"That book sticking out of your purse."

"What's the big deal?"

He looked at her as if the answer were obvious. "You don't even take time for lunch," he said, "never mind a break to read."

"Research. Have you heard of it?"

"What's to research?"

"*Titanic.*" She pulled the book out of her bag and flipped through the pages. "There's a bunch of statistics at the front. And in the back," she said, stopping at the page she was looking for, "there are survivor accounts." She dropped the book in front of Morgan and pointed to the open page. "Look. This one's written by a third-class passenger."

"So?"

"Look at the author."

"Jakob Tellemann. Again. So what?"

Melika let out a long sigh. "Don't you remember doing surveillance on Blake Tellemann's funeral, the guy killed at the launch?"

"Yeah."

"His full name was Blake Jakob Tellemann. I remember because I joked about it. *Blake Jake.* Jake short for Jakob? Blake and Jake rhyming? This ring any bells?"

"Yeah, yeah, I remember." Morgan stuck his nose in the air, and Melika thought it gave him a distinctively self-righteous, haughty look. Like the French. "Personally," he said, "I thought you were very insensitive."

Melika grabbed a piece of paper from the garbage, crumpled it up, and pitched it at her partner. "You laughed, too," she said and cursed for missing the mark.

"Regardless," he said. "What, if anything, does this have to do with our investigation?"

Now that she thought about it, Melika didn't know. "Nothing, I guess."

"Where'd you get the book?"
"Harwood."
"A gift? This *is* serious."
"It's not a gift. It's sort of a loan."
"You stole it?"
"I didn't steal it. I just forgot to leave it."
Morgan sat up, closed the book, and handed it back to Melika. "Harwood's pretty far up the food chain at Klipper, right?"
"Yeah."
"All right. Take him out for lunch. Ask for a tour of the ship. Give him his book back. Whatever excuse you want to use to get to know him."
"No way, Morgan—not even if I wanted to. Cops and civilians don't mix. You know that."
"I'm not saying you gotta make it personal. We could use someone on the inside to keep an eye on Janus. Harwood would be perfect."
"He won't go for it."
"Don't tell him."
Her leg was fidgeting. She forced it to stop. "I don't think it's a good idea."
"Have I ever led you down the wrong alley?"
"Always."
"When?"
"All right," she admitted. "You've never led me down the wrong alley."
"Of course I haven't. I know what I'm doing. They don't call me Columbo for nothing."
"We call you Columbo because of the way you dress."
"I like my raincoat."

"It's not just the coat."

Morgan glanced at the clock. "I gotta go," he said, standing. "I'm taking my wife to Chez George's for her birthday."

"Wish her happy birthday for me," Melika said.

Melika watched Morgan leave. She wondered whether this little scheme of his would actually net some actionable information. Morgan was smart, that was for sure. A pain in the ass but one of the few people she felt comfortable with. He'd take a bullet for her, just like she'd take one for him. But it was more than that. If she ever met her father, she'd want him to be just like Morgan.

Leaning back in her chair, she closed her eyes, thinking of Abram's black and white photograph. Typically, she never noticed things like that. She knew about crime and the pathology of a criminal's psyche, but she didn't take time to stop and smell the roses. Obviously, Abram was different. He'd seen something other than dead people in an old cemetery and had the talent to get it on film. Or in pixels, or however stills were captured nowadays.

She drummed her fingers on the cover of his book, once again staring at the wall.

All right, Morgan, she thought, sitting up. *You win.*

Abram picked up the receiver on the first ring.

"Mr. Harwood ... Abram. It's Detective Jones."

"Melika, right?"

"Yes." Her knee was shaking again. She really needed to give up caffeine.

"What can I do for you?"

"I was hoping for a tour of the yards," she said. "And *Titan's Sister*. It slipped my mind earlier."

Abram cleared his throat. "Sure. I'm not back to work until Monday, but I can certainly show you around before then."

"How about now?"

"Now?"

"Yeah. My partner knocked off early, so I'm free for a few hours."

He hesitated. *He's either checking the time or thinking of a way to beg off.*

"I'm not sure," he said. "The yards won't be a problem. But we can't tour the whole ship because of the fire damage."

"That's fine."

"Okay. I'll catch a cab and meet you there in twenty minutes."

"Forget the cab. I'll pick you up."

Chapter Seven

"You hungry?" Abram asked, taking Melika's hard hat and safety goggles.

"Yeah," she said. "A little bit."

He hadn't realized how long it had taken them to tour the ship and yards. But his stomach had started growling at least an hour ago, and it hadn't stopped since. "I know this great little diner on the wharf," he said, showing her out of Klipper's reception area. "Margaret's Cafe. It has everything. Seafood, burgers, sandwiches."

Melika buttoned up her jacket. The sun had set, and a cool wind was coming off the ocean. "Sure. I'll buy. I'll expense it."

"Still on the clock, huh?"

She shook her head. "No, no. You're right. We'd better go Dutch."

"It's funny," Abram said when they reached her vehicle. "Your car looks exactly like the white Ford sedan that sits outside Klipper's yards."

She got behind the wheel and stretched across the bench seat to unlock the front passenger door. She'd changed into jeans and runners from the business attire she'd worn earlier in the day, but she still had on the dressy, loose-fitting top. While she fumbled to open his door, he had an unobstructed view down her blouse.

"It's a popular model," Melika said as Abram settled into the passenger seat. "Common color."

"True." He struggled to latch his seat belt, reminding himself they were talking about the Ford sedan.

She started the car, dropped it into drive, and glanced in his direction. "Why? You think someone's watching?"

He smiled. "Yeah. You."

Had it not been for the pale lights of the dash highlighting her soft features, he wouldn't have noticed the slight stiffening of her lips and eyes, confirming he was right.

"I wouldn't read too much into it," she said and pulled onto the road.

Speaking of reading, he wondered if he should ask her about the book she'd taken from his condo.

Something beeped, drawing his attention to the dash. "Shit. Is that the time?"

"Yeah. Five to seven. Why?"

"Umm, well," he said, "what about a ballpark frank for dinner?"

"Huh?"

"Hot dog."

"Yeah. I know what a ballpark frank is."

"I told my dad I'd meet him at the Marlins game. It's spring training."

She slowed but didn't brake, looking at Abram for longer than he thought was safe for someone behind the wheel. "I haven't been to a ball game in ages," she said.

"They're playing the Yankees."

"I hate the Yankees."

"So does everybody else. So it should be a good game."

A driver behind blew the horn while Melika decided whether she wanted to turn or continue down the road for the ballpark. She glanced in the rearview mirror. "Asshole," she grumbled.

"Or you can drop me at the bus stop," Abram said.

The car behind sped past, horn blaring. Melika floored her car and flicked on the siren and strobes. "Jerk," she said, hitting ninety before slowing to sit on the guy's bumper. He pulled over with little room to maneuver. Instead of steering in behind, Melika cruised past. It wasn't until she settled back to her typical speed of five to ten miles over the limit that she turned off the lights and siren.

If he didn't have bandaged hands, Abram would've been hanging on for dear life. He tried not to sound shaken. "That guy probably shit his pants."

"He should thank me. I could've been some enraged lunatic with a gun. Bang, he's dead."

* * * *

They sat in the first set of bleachers, Clay on one side of Abram and Melika on the other. Clay leaned toward Abram and whispered, "I can't believe you brought a cop to a ball game."

Melika waved at the guy selling snacks. "Hey," she yelled. "Toss us a bag of peanuts."

"Classy," Clay said.

"Pop, shhh."

Clay dug in his pocket. "You get the beers. I'll get the hot dogs."

Abram nodded.

"I assume the detective wants a dog," Clay said.

"You can call me Melika," she said. "And make it two."

Clay screwed up his face but didn't hesitate to pull out more money.

The game got underway with a base hit on the first pitch. By the third inning, the Marlins were down by two but had the bases loaded. Clay was standing. Melika and Abram were on the edge of their seats. The pitcher wound up, Abram reached for some nuts, missed, hit Melika's hand, and spilled them all over her lap. Instinctively, he rushed to pick them up. When he realized where he was headed, he froze. Melika jumped to her feet, the nuts flying.

"Son of a—" Clay said, dropping into his chair.

"What?" Abram turned quickly.

"We struck out. That's what."

"Oh." Abram checked on Melika. She had sat back down, but her head was turned the other way.

Abram rubbed his neck, cleared his throat, and thought about going to the concession for more beer, but he decided he shouldn't leave Pop and Melika alone. He sat, relieved when Melika struck up a conversation about the shipyard. Women were seldom interested in the nitty-gritty of his work, and he wondered if she was just being polite. But that didn't suit her style.

The remainder of the game was a bust, and the Marlins added to their losing streak.

"You guys want a ride home?" Melika asked.

Abram glanced at his father.

"No thanks," Clay said. "I'm not sitting in the back of a cop car."

Melika headed for the stairs. She waved. "See you later, then. Thanks for the hot dogs, Mr. Harwood."

They watched her until she was out of sight.
Clay elbowed Abram. "Nice-looking woman."
"Yeah."
"Too bad she's a cop."
"Yeah." Abram rubbed his chin.
"You can probably still catch up with her."
Abram hesitated but shook his head. "You haven't seen her drive."

Chapter Eight

In the shadow of a full moon, Abram and Floyd, the yard superintendent, watched the red, green, and white lights of the *Sister* fade into the darkness of a mid-April evening. She was sailing down the coast to Algo's pier at Port Canaveral. Tomorrow, a month and a half after the dock fire, she'd take on passengers and begin her maiden voyage.

"Right on time," Floyd said.

Abram rubbed the back of his neck. Except for the scars on his hands, he'd recovered from the fire with no lasting effects. "They shouldn't be sailing with only four out of the six boilers commissioned," he said.

The superintendent laughed. "Harwood, sorry to break this to you. You're just the welder, not the captain. He doesn't give a damn that she can't run at top speed without those boilers. Nor does Janus. It's their ship now."

The night was cold. The Weather Channel had warned of frost, the low temperatures threatening a bumper crop of Valencia oranges.

Abram shook his head. "It's not about speed. The ship is fully automated, programmed to operate with six boilers. It's like a V6 running on only four cylinders."

"It's not a car. It's a ship. A hell of a big ship. Nobody is gonna notice."

"Still, it should be right."

"You're a perfectionist, Harwood. One of the few." He slapped Abram on the back. "Good working with ya." Floyd turned and left.

Abram checked his watch. "Shit." He was late.

*   *   *   *

An hour later, he had showered, pressed a shirt, and cleaned his dress pants with a lint catcher. Thanks to his father, Abram left the condo with his shoes polished and necktie straight.

When he reached Richard's Gourmet, Abram was ten minutes early. And hungry. Not just for food. How long since he'd been—actually *been*—with a woman? Too long.

He and Melika had kept in touch since the Marlins lost to the Yankees, taking in a few more baseball games, meeting for lunch on a couple occasions and going for several early morning jogs around the park. She was a hard runner and had no trouble matching Abram's pace.

On one occasion, they'd met for an impromptu dinner, Melika not wanting to indulge in anything fancier than Denny's.

Tonight, she had picked Richard's, a quiet, intimate place and one of Abram's favorites. She said it was a bon voyage celebration. He assumed that meant more than dinner.

He checked in with the restaurant's maitre d', then found a chair but didn't sit. He tapped his watch.

He sensed, more than saw, a change in the room. A beautiful woman in high-heeled shoes and an elegant, low-cut black dress and jacket was making her way toward him. She caught the attention of every man she passed. Even the women looked her way, most with varying degrees of envy.

"I'm not late, am I?" Melika said, a little too loudly for the ambiance she'd created.

"No, you're perfect," Abram said. "I mean your timing's perfect."

"Great." She scanned the room. "I've never been here before, but they say it's a nice place. Is our table ready?"

"I think so."

The host led them to a secluded table by the window. The lights of several distant ships sparkled on the flat surface of the ocean.

They ordered red wine and Caesar salad to start.

"So," Melika said after the waiter took away the menus. "You seem excited. I'm guessing *Titan's Sister* finished her last-minute trials without a hitch."

"Janus is pleased."

"You're not?" Melika leaned back while the waiter dropped off a basket of warm rolls and a sampling of assorted butters.

"She's got some bugs," Abram said, trying the greenest of the various spreads. "Nothing major. A couple more days, she would've been perfect."

"Nothing's perfect, Abram." Melika washed down a large bite of roll with several sips of wine. "I'm starving. I can't remember when I last had something."

"I know," Abram said. "It's been a while for me, too."

"Are you going to check out any of the hot spots?"

"Hot spots?"

"Sightseeing. When the ship docks in England."

"Oh, right. Yeah, I'm thinking of renting a car. Pop has a few places he wants to go to."

"How'd you finally talk him into it?"

Abram refilled their glasses. "I told him what you said. Lots of rich, widowed women will be on board."

"Lots of rich, widowed, *white* women were my exact words."

"Yeah, I know. He realizes that."

Their salads arrived. The waiter offered to serve it in two small bowls, but they shared a plate.

"I like your father," Melika said, digging in. "I'm glad he's forgotten about our clash in your hospital room."

"He can't hold a grudge against someone who roots for the Marlins. Besides, you're from our hometown. He thinks that's good karma." Abram forked an anchovy. "Now, your partner, Morgan. He's a different story."

"Completely understandable," she said, flicking her anchovies Abram's way.

For the main course, Melika had the pasta of the day, and Abram had the house specialty, steak and lobster tails.

They were finishing their cappuccinos when she started fumbling with something under the table.

"My pager's vibrating," she said.

Abram stood when Melika got up. He didn't take his eyes off her body as she twisted through the tables to find a phone.

"Don't be long," he whispered.

*   *   *   *

Melika cursed herself for leaving her cell at home. Luckily, the restaurant had some pay phones. After several minutes of digging impatiently through her purse, she finally found enough change and made the call. "Okay, Morgan," she said when he picked up the phone. "What's going on?"

"*Titan's Sister* just dropped anchor in Waterdown."

"What? Why? There were no scheduled stops en route to Algo's port."

"I know."

"Is there something wrong with the ship?"

"Nope. They're taking on cargo," Morgan said.

"What kind of cargo? Did you check the manifest?"

"Yep, I checked the manifest," her partner said. "Nothing's listed from Waterdown. All provisions are supposed to be loaded tonight and tomorrow at Algo's gate."

"That's what I thought." She lowered her voice despite the noise of the restaurant. "Contraband?"

"Not that simple. My CI in Waterdown tells me it's sand."

"That's ridiculous. I know Janus is crazy. But shipping sand from one beach to another?"

"There's something else you should know."

"What?" she asked.

"You're booked on the ship."

"What ship?"

"*Titan's Sister*, of course."

"What!"

"You heard me," Morgan said. "God knows what Janus is up to. Chief wants us to keep an eye on him."

Melika felt a headache coming on. "Why don't you go on the ship?"

"Not without my wife. Besides, I already got the ticket in your name."

"How? I thought *Titan's Sister* was booked solid."

"It is. But I know someone who knows someone. Consider it a free vacation. It's been six years since you took time off."

"Come on, Morgan. A cruise? Just to watch Janus?"

"What? You worried you'll hit an iceberg?"

"Of course not."

"Then what's the problem?"

Sighing heavily, Melika lowered the phone to think, but her brain was struggling to stay afloat in a pool of alcohol. She put the receiver back to her ear. "What am I going to tell Abram? He's on that ship."

"Tell him you wanted to go on the cruise with him."

"He'll wonder why we just didn't shack up in his cabin."

"You've got strict morals."

"No, I don't. Listen, Morgan, I'm not prepared for this. I'm half in the bag."

"I would've told you sooner, but you forgot your cell phone, remember?"

"Yeah, yeah." She checked her watch. "Shit, it's nearly midnight."

"Look, if you want, leave it to me. I'll find out as much as I can and brief you on the way to the terminal tomorrow."

She blew out a long breath. "Fine," she said. "I'll see you then."

Melika replaced the receiver and ran her hand over her hair. She tugged at the ends. Looking down, she wondered why, with all the comfortable clothes in her closet, she'd bought this dress. She stepped out of her high heels. Her feet hurt. And the nylons, though advertised as soft, silky, and sheer, were starting to bind and itch. Very impractical for a cop.

She pulled her shoulders back, tugged at her bra's tight elastic band, and returned to the restaurant.

"Sorry, Abram," she said. "I gotta go."

Chapter Nine

Sailing day—finally. Abram pulled his truck up to the kiosk at the terminal's entrance. He and Clay were early, so there wasn't a line of cars waiting to be let in. But the protesters, waving their placards, were distracting street traffic and doing their best to slow things down. Abram dropped off their bags and parked. They took the shuttle to the terminal building, eventually clearing security and checking in with the cruise line.

They were among the first in the waiting area, a long and narrow room with windows overlooking the dock. Every seat was darkened by the *Sister*'s heavy shadow. Abram and Clay sat near the middle, Abram scanning the ship bow to stern. "She's pretty impressive, huh, Pop?"

Clay fiddled with his carry-on. After stuffing his passport and key card in a deep pocket, he sat up, glanced at the ship, nodded, and looked at Abram. "Son, I've got this nagging sense that I've forgotten something."

"Cognitive dysphasia."

"What?"

"That's what they've coined it. A nice way to say you're absent-minded. Like the rest of us."

"Christ, pretty soon everything will be a disease." Clay suddenly raised his forefinger in the air. "I've got it. The iron. Did you unplug it?"

"Ah ..."

Clay hit him on the arm. "Relax. I was joking." He tugged at his shirt collar. "You oughta try polyester. Never have to worry about the iron."

"I don't think so," Abram said, eyeing Pop's yellow and slightly shiny shirt. "Hey, what's that?"

"What?"

"That pendant you're wearing."

Clay picked it up, holding it in his fist. "Don't read anything into it, son."

"I thought you got rid of it. After Mom left."

"Nope. You never give away your luck. Good or bad."

Abram shook his head. "Amulets don't work. You know that, right?"

"Of course. I just wanted to dress up a bit." Clay flipped his hand in the *Sister*'s direction. "I mean, look at the ship. It sure is decked out."

Abram took a long look at the ship. *Pop is right. It looks overdecorated. Janus is probably compensating for the lack of fanfare at the launch.*

Abram turned back to his father. Clay had tucked his charm back under his shirt. *Thankfully, some things never change. The things you can count on.* He said, "I appreciate you tagging along, Pop."

"I know it's important to you."

Abram nodded and checked out their fellow passengers. The waiting room was filling up. Carrying trays of hors d'oeuvres and beverages, several waiters in white jackets meandered through the crowd. A nice touch, Abram thought, catching the eye of one of the waiters.

Two hours later, Clay was on his third beer, and Abram was still munching on hors d'oeuvres and nursing his first beer.

"It's a good thing the drinks are free," Clay said. "Or I'd be getting pretty irritated by now."

"Yeah. I wonder what the hold-up is."

Clay got up. "Watch my bag. I gotta go walk the dog."

"Sure." Abram moved the carry-on closer to him. When he sat back up, he couldn't believe who was standing in front of him. "Holy shit!" he said.

Melika struggled with three bags. "Nice to see you, too." She didn't crack a smile. "Here, help me with these things."

He reached for what looked like an overnight case, but she pulled it away and handed him her oversized purse.

"You're booked on this cruise?" he asked.

Melika nodded. With the overnight case in one hand, and her papers and the ship's card in the other, she fought without success to keep the straps of her suit bag from falling down her arm. Abram lifted them back onto her shoulder.

She let out a sigh and looked around the room. "I'd hoped everybody would be boarded by now."

"No. Some sort of delay."

"I hear the captain's pissed because Janus let a bunch of reporters tag along for the ship's final inspection." Melika noticed Abram's drink. "Where'd you get that?"

"Algo's handing them out like candy."

Melika ordered spring water from a passing waiter. "Anyway," she said. "The captain's taking his sweet time with the inspection, being extra thorough."

Abram chuckled. "That'll drive Janus nuts."

"Yep." Melika looked around after taking several swallows of her drink. "Where's your father?"

"Relieving himself of his first three beers. How'd you get a ticket? The cruise was sold out months ago."

"I know people who know people."

"You bought a ticket from a scalper? That's illegal."

"Shhh, Abram. Keep your voice down."

"This makes no sense. I thought you hated cruise ships, especially the *Sister*."

"And I thought you'd be glad to see me."

"I am. I am. Come on, let's sit."

"Wait." She watched a waiter pass nearby. "I know that guy. He's a goof."

Abram glanced at the waiter, a pubescent-looking man who hardly seemed a threat. "What's the big deal?"

"Listen. Let's just keep the fact that I'm a cop between the two of us. You know what I mean?"

He shook his head. "No, not really." Nor was Abram sure it mattered.

The night before, he didn't get anywhere near Melika's bed. Today, looking at her tight jeans and scanty T-shirt highlighting her sexy curves, Abram found it hard to think of anything other than the second chance Lady Luck had given him. She appeared cold and he offered her his windbreaker for her shoulders, but her you've-got-to-be-kidding look reminded him that she'd sucker-punched chivalry ages ago.

Then Pop was back, and they were saying hello, Melika explaining that Abram had talked her into coming.

"Hey, you two," Abram said. "They're boarding. Let's go."

Not surprisingly, there was a rush to the gangway. But as passengers fanned out into the *Sister*'s reception area on D deck, the pace slowed, the décor embracing them in a calmer, more peaceful world. Tapestries of floral designs, scenic countryside, and boar hunting hung on Jacobean-styled white walls. Persian rugs covered the light tile flooring. And filling the room, without overcrowding it, were polished wood tables, wing chairs, high-backed love seats, lofty, potted palms, and jardinières of ferns or fresh flowers.

Abram and Melika, with Clay not far behind, made their way toward the elevators tucked behind the grand staircase. The curved, graceful staircase was an imposing part of the ship, extending six decks from E deck to the boat deck, where a huge circular dome provided a flood of natural light. A spacious and open area surrounded the staircase, giving Abram the impression of a ballroom. He could picture a debutante at the top of the steps.

"Where's your cabin?" he asked Melika.

"E deck," she said.

"Steerage accommodations."

"What?"

"You're third-class."

"Like hell I am."

An elevator arrived going up. "We're on B," Abram said, following his father in. "Let's meet back here in half an hour."

Abram and Clay didn't have far to go to find their suites. They had adjoining cabins on the starboard side, numbers B-57 and B-58, the third and fourth doors aft of the grand staircase.

As Clay headed off to inspect his cabin, Abram looked around his. It was a big stateroom, offering substantially more living area than the typical modern cruise ship. The décor was either Queen Anne or Italian Renaissance, Abram wasn't sure. His preference would've been a contemporary style, but it wouldn't have been true to *Titanic*. Fortunately, the room's large open-out windows provided sunlight and a fresh breeze, offsetting the cabin's stiff parlor look.

He sat on the bed, testing the mattress. At first, he thought it was comfortable. But the longer he sat, the stranger he felt. He stood and took a step away, a chill running down his spine. He hadn't considered who had occupied this cabin on *Titanic*. Nor did he know whether they had lived or died the night she sank. Abram chided himself for not bringing one of Blake's books for reference. The one Melika had stolen from his condo would've been perfect.

"Hey, Abram," Clay said, parading into Abram's room through the interconnecting door. "Let's go find Melika and all those rich widows you were talking about."

After they'd met up with Melika, they headed topside and settled into deck chairs.

It wasn't long until the boarding gate was closed and an obligatory lifeboat drill called. Everyone located his or her muster station quicker than expected. Abram figured the passengers on the *Sister* understood better than most the danger of not confirming a place in a lifeboat.

As the ship eased from her berth, Melika said, "Look," and pointed at a group of people on the dock.

Abram strained to see. "They're waving good-bye."

"No, they're not. They're pointing at something." She turned her back to the rail. "Look. At the top of the first funnel."

Abram shielded his eyes. He wondered if he should have them checked. "I don't see ... hey, there's a guy up there!"

"No shit!"

"He's yelling something," Abram said.

Clay cupped his ears. "I can't hear a damn thing over the ship's horn."

By now, most of the passengers on deck were watching the man on the funnel. A lot of them were cheering.

Melika crossed her arms. "I don't get it."

The man next to her moved closer, nearer than Abram liked. "It's the same as 1912," he said. "Someone from the engine department scurried up the fake funnel as a harmless little prank. Back then, the fake funnel was the furthest aft not the furthest forward."

Melika looked at Abram.

Abram shrugged.

"Okay," Melika said to the man. "Thanks." She shifted toward Abram, away from the man.

The guy didn't take the hint and spoke louder. "It's funny," he said. "Many passengers on *Titanic* said it was a bad omen. That it secured their terrible fate."

Clay let out a long breath. "Oh, great."

"Pop, it's not a big deal," Abram said.

"Show's over," Melika interrupted. "He's gone."

"Good." Abram checked the time. People were already heading below to get dressed for dinner. "I don't know about you guys," he said. "But I'm not real hungry yet."

"Me either," Clay said. "Too many snacks in the terminal."

Melika took one more look at the funnel then leaned against the rail. "What do you suggest?"

Abram pointed toward the stern. "There's the À La Carte Restaurant on B deck. You can get as much or as little as you want."

"Perfect," Melika said.

* * * *

The À La Carte Restaurant was bright and airy, Melika thought fifteen minutes later as she sat at the bar with Abram and Clay waiting for a table.

The men ordered cocktails. Melika stuck to water. She wouldn't be able to face alcohol for a while. Not after last night at Richard's.

She rubbed her eyes. She was tired but had accomplished a lot already. She'd found out the names of the stewards and stewardesses who served Janus's room, and she'd met the chief purser. Even better, after freshening-up for dinner, she discovered that *Titan's Sister* had hired a cabin boy. Obviously, it was another throwback to the early 1900s. Janus must've pulled quite a few strings to get around child labor laws.

The boy was thirteen, dark-haired, not tall, not skinny, and not shy, but certainly well mannered. Melika noticed him on the boat deck, hustling out the crew door with papers in hand. She casually stepped in his way, knocking them both off their feet. He apologized repeatedly for his clumsiness as he helped her back up. She took the opportunity to strike up a conversation.

"What's your name, kid?"

"Please don't report me. The captain's mad enough."

"No, no." She glanced at the tag pinned to his chest. "Michael Reyes, right? You part of the crew?"

"I run their errands, ma'am."

"Call me Melika. What's the captain upset about?"

"It was that guy." Michael waved toward the funnel. "Mr. Janus thought it was great. But the captain, he wants an explanation. He's got everybody looking for the guy. You sure you're okay?"

"Yep. Thanks," she said and headed to the À La Carte Restaurant to met Abram.

She elbowed Abram, nearly spilling his drink. "What do you think about funnel man?" she asked.

"Who?"

"The guy up in the funnel, waving at everyone when we left."

He shrugged. "I don't know."

"I wonder if Janus hired the guy."

"Probably. He hasn't forgotten any other detail about *Titanic*."

"That we know of."

"True."

Finally, they were seated. The food was almost as good as Richard's. Melika finished her coffee and stretched.

"Too tired to take a walk around the ship?" Abram asked.

After three cups of coffee, she had energy to burn, but a walk was not what she had in mind.

Clay stood, excusing himself. "Okay if I lock up the adjoining doors?" he asked as he left. "You know how I like the TV loud."

Abram agreed, then turned to Melika. "How about we make it a quick walk?"

She stood. "Okay, a quick one," she said. "Let me change first."

They agreed to meet in twenty minutes. Melika grabbed an elevator, got off at E deck, and hustled to her cabin, key card in hand. Twenty minutes didn't give her much time, but it would have to do if she didn't want to make Abram suspicious.

Inside her cabin, she peeled off her pants and shirt, threw them on the bed, and opened her suitcase. Rummaging through her clothes, she grabbed a pair of black jeans, a dark top—not too wrinkled—and a tweed jacket. In the zippered part of her suitcase were her runners. From her overnight case, she picked out a few items. Though she didn't figure she'd need it, Melika also grabbed her gun, a Glock 17. She was surprised they'd let her have it, but it was hidden right where Morgan had said it would be.

Within two minutes, she was jogging down the aisle on her way back to the elevator.

She stopped on A deck and headed past the elevators toward the bow. She hoped she remembered the deck layouts she had studied earlier in the day. With a fifty/fifty chance, she took the corridor on the port side.

To her left were the staterooms. The other side was wallpapered in a beige print and adorned with pictures of various landscapes. Behind this wall was the base of the forward funnel where funnel man would've gained access.

Near the end of the corridor, Melika found what she was looking for. Opposite the last stateroom was a door marked "Ventilation Room, Authorized Personnel Only." Glancing over her shoulder to ensure nobody was in sight, Melika hurriedly pulled a thin instrument from her pocket. She jammed the tool into the door lock, turned the knob, and hurried inside.

It was pitch black. She stood perfectly still, giving her eyes a chance to adjust. She could sense movement above and suspected it was the large ventilation fans slowly rotating, the warm air from below moving toward the colder environment outside. She couldn't hear the motors, but above the steady sound of the ship, the power supplies hummed loudly.

Melika reached behind her back, pulled her Mini Maglite from her waistband and clicked it on. The room sparkled, the way only a brand-new ventilation compartment could.

Training her flashlight on the ceiling, she saw the fans, their large blades cutting its beam, creating a slow strobe effect in the room. In that eerie illumination, Melika spotted the hatch that led to the top of the funnel. The cover was slightly ajar.

She took a step forward, still focusing the beam of the Mini Mag on the partly open hatch, and bumped into something on the floor.

The clatter echoed loudly in the shaft. She looked down, more concerned about the noise than a scraped shin.

She'd tripped on a stepladder. Obviously, it was the instrument used to gain access to the hatch. The ladder had been knocked over, and either it was too heavy to stash quickly or funnel man simply didn't care if it was found. Melika bent over, attempting to ascertain its weight. It was aluminum. She could lift it and, if she had to, even set it up to see if anything of interest lay beyond the hatch. Right now, she wanted to continue her cursory inspection of the room.

She straightened up, holding the light near her shoulder.

She froze.

Her sense of smell had kicked in.

It had only been a few hours since funnel man had made his appearance, but the odor that mingled in the hot air of the room was unmistakable.

She continued forward, her gun steady and close to her body, her light sweeping the room. Directing the beam behind the ventilation shaft, she spotted a heavy blanket covering something in the corner.

With one quick movement, Melika pulled it away, and stood, pointing both the sight of her gun and the beam of her Mini Mag into the corner.

"Police, don't move," she said, her voice strong but low.

No movement. None.

She had found funnel man. He was sitting against the wall with his knees against his chest and his eyes open. His head was bent awkwardly to one side.

With her gun steady, she took a step forward and bent over, the pounding in her ears beginning to subside.

Melika reached into the corner. Her hands on cool flesh, she confirmed what she had suspected. Funnel man was dead.

She locked the safety on her gun and assessed the unfortunate man.

He was dressed like one of *Titanic*'s black gang, a coal stoker she'd seen pictures of when leafing through Abram's book. Dark pants, a scant T-shirt, boots, and nothing more except the grease smeared on his face. She looked closer and noticed his shaven, though toughened face, clean fingernails, but crooked fingers, and hard, yet uncalloused hands. He was a passenger, or at least not a maintenance man or engineer from the ship's crew.

She patted him down as a matter of routine and checked his pockets. Nothing was on him except a small piece of paper that she stuffed in her jeans to study later.

Melika took one more quick look at the body. She moved his head, looking for any sign of contusions. A large bruise was evident, but there was minimal blood and no evidence of a struggle. The probable cause of death was brain hemorrhaging due to the fall.

She placed the blanket over the dead man, ensuring his face was covered. She couldn't let the body fester. She'd notify the captain and let him deal with it. Maybe they'd head to the nearest port. Melika wondered how the side-trip would affect Janus's plans.

Securing the Glock in the back of her jeans, she stood and checked her watch.

It was time to get back.

* * * *

Seated in the foyer of the boat deck's grand staircase, Abram found it hard to believe that under all the woodwork, expensive carpet, marble flooring, and gold fixtures was the metal skeleton he and his crew had welded together.

Undoubtedly, this area was the ship's most elaborate.

The huge circular skylight was supported with patterned wrought ironwork and bathed in a muted glow by the gold and crystal fixture in the middle. On each deck down to the reception area on D, the staircase was surrounded by a large and elaborate room with oak paneled walls, light-colored marble floors, and balconies overlooking the level below.

Particularly interesting, Abram thought as he watched for Melika, was the woodwork on the staircase wall leading down to the next deck. Sculpted into the oak were two goddess-like figures. A crown was at their feet and between them was a clock. Melika was nearly fifteen minutes late.

He couldn't imagine what was keeping her.

It certainly wasn't mulling over clothes and taking time putting them on, he decided when he spotted her laboring up the stairs. Her outfit was too dark, her shirt-tail was out, and she looked too exhausted to mount another step. It wasn't at all what he'd expected when she said she was going to get changed.

"You okay?" he asked.

"Yeah, fine." She dropped into a chair beside him. "I thought I'd get some exercise. Man, this ship is bigger than it looks."

"Really? Most people think it looks pretty big."

"You know what I mean. It's a figure of speech."

"I thought we were going to get some exercise together. Remember? A quick walk?"

"I need something to drink first."

They headed to the lounge on the promenade deck and found a quiet corner by the window.

Abram ordered two cognacs, but soon realized he'd have to drink both. Melika only wanted water, cold but with no ice.

He finished the first brandy quickly. Feeling his muscles relax, he settled back in the chair. With one elbow on the armrest, his hand holding his chin, he picked up his second drink, gently swirling the amber liquid as he studied Melika's face. Beads of perspiration had collected on her forehead and upper lip.

She leaned on the table, checking out the handful of patrons scattered around the room, her eyes always moving but never settling on Abram.

"You know," he said. "I'm getting mixed messages here."

Finally, she focused on him. "What do you mean?"

"Last night. Tonight. I'm not sure what you want."

"What I want?"

"I thought we had some sort of connection. That we were both ready for the next step."

She rubbed her forehead, then rubbed her hands together, not quickly and without thought, but deliberately like *that was the end of that.* She took a long drink of water before speaking. "Abram, listen," she said, wiping her mouth. "Richard's was a mistake."

Though he was fairly certain his heart had lost a couple of beats, Abram tried to maintain a façade of aloofness. "Really?"

"Yeah. I mean, that person wasn't me." She waved her hand up and down her body. "This is me," she said. "A cop. That's what I know. That comes first."

"Comes first?" He laughed.

"It's not a joke."

She wasn't smiling. In fact, her seriousness displayed something Abram had never seen before. "You're scared," he said.

"Scared? I'm not scared of anything."

"Bullshit. You're scared. And hiding behind that badge. You nearly admitted as much."

"You have no idea what it's like being a cop."

"And you have no idea what it's like to be within arm's reach of a beautiful woman and not be able to get any closer." His tone was strong, forceful, the sentence out of his mouth before he could think about it. Then he too straightened up, narrowing his eyes. "Or do you?"

"What in hell does that mean?"

"I saw the way some of the women were looking at you last night. You didn't seem to mind. In fact—"

"Christ, Abram." She sat back, crossing her arms and shaking her head. When she returned her gaze, she was still shaking her head but had lowered her voice. "You men are all the same," she said. "So high and mighty. You've decided I'm gay simply because I'm not crawling all over you at the first opportunity."

Abram was confused. He thought he'd done everything right. "Then what's the last six weeks been about?"

She didn't have an immediate answer. Finally, she said, "It won't work, Abram. It was never going to work." She paused for a sip of water, swallowed hard, and had to clear her throat before continuing. "You see," she said, pushing away the glass. "Morgan and I needed someone on the inside. Someone intimate with the shipyard's activities." She waited for Abram to respond. When he didn't, she said, "I'm sorry."

Abram didn't give Melika the benefit of any change of expression. Instead, he asked simply, "Did you get what you needed, Melika?"

She nodded. "Yes."

"I'm glad one of us did." He ordered another cognac—a double.

"Maybe I should go," she said.

He grabbed her arm. He expected her to pull away. She didn't.

Instead, she put her hand on his as if everything was going to be okay. "Talk to your cabin steward," she said. "Maybe he can hook you up with someone."

Abram rolled his eyes. "Oh, yeah, right. Escorts on a ship like this."

"You're so naive, Abram." She pulled away, turned and headed for the door.

Naive? he thought. If anyone didn't understand the world, it was Melika. She was so good at distancing herself from it. Yeah, that was exactly what was going on. And he knew just how to show her.

She was nearly out of the lounge when he called to her. "Detective Jones," he yelled.

She immediately hustled back. "Quiet, Abram. We had a deal, remember?"

"Right," he said. "I'm not supposed to tell people you're a cop."

"No, you're not."

Abram feigned a chuckle. "You really don't get it, do you? Not that it matters, but I know why you're on board. And I'm not the only one who's figured it out." He watched her eyes. *She wants to tell me where to go.*

She pulled out a chair and sat on the edge. "What are you suggesting?"

He shrugged.

"If you know something—"

"I know you're not as clever as you think you are." He leaned back, crossing his legs, getting comfortable with his cognac once again.

"Abram, I'm not in the mood."

"You've made that clear."

"For games. I'm not in the mood for games."

"Nor am I." He offered nothing more.

She turned in her chair to get up. "I'm leaving," she said as if it were a threat. But she didn't stand.

Abram remained quiet.

Making fists and hitting them together several times, eventually she asked, "Do you know something or not?"

"Let me say this." He set down his glass. "I'm not the one at this table who's naive."

"What does *that* mean?"

"It's not Janus you need to watch."

"Who then?"

"My dear Melika." He took her hands, drawing her close enough to kiss. But he didn't. "Trust me," he said, hoping she could feel his breath on her face. "Janus isn't the threat." He shook his head. "Uh-uh. It's me, Melika. I'm the one you need to watch."

Chapter Ten

Melika flicked off her shoes and flattened out on her bed, ignoring the phone's message light. Morgan, likely. *In a minute*, she thought and shut her eyes tightly, draping her arm over her face.

Damn Harwood. Damn Morgan! After all, he got me into this mess. Hook up with Abram for the sake of their investigation. Bullshit.

She picked up the phone and punched out the number for her partner's home. A teenager answered. Loud music in the background. *Shit.* "Sorry, wrong number," she said and took a minute to calm herself. She tried again, this time slowing down a bit.

Morgan answered on the fourth ring, his voice low, groggy. "It's late. Where've you been?"

"Don't ask."

"Just a second."

Melika heard a soft sound, the movement of blankets likely, followed by a creak. She guessed that Morgan had been in bed and was moving to a quiet corner so he wouldn't wake his wife. *How long have Morgan and Nancy been married? A millennium, give or take. And he still cares enough not to disturb her.*

When Morgan came back, he said, "Guess who picked up a brand new Mercedes today?"

"Not you. Not on your salary." She sat up and undid the top two buttons of her blouse, trying to get comfortable.

"Fire Marshall Quinn."

"No way!"

"I knew that would lighten your mood. Two hours after you set sail, he went to the dealership out at Oakpark and paid cash for a 500C."

"Man, people are stupid. That's so obviously suspect. How'd you find out?"

"The salesman's a buddy of mine."

She pulled her feet up close, crossing her legs. "You got buddies everywhere."

"Tricks of the trade."

"Gotta love 'em."

"It was such fun," he said. "I pulled in Quinn's driveway right behind him and put on the strobes for effect. I showed him my cuffs, threatening to arrest him right then and there if he didn't talk. He sang like a bird."

"Scared shitless, huh?"

"Yep."

"So what'd he say?"

"Get this," Morgan said. "Despite what he reported, Quinn found traces of an accelerant in Harwood's welding tent. He also discovered remnants of a matchbook and a cigarette butt, an amateur's makeshift fuse. Combine that with an open propane tank, and you've got yourself a nice start to a fire."

"So it *was* arson."

"Quinn said it wasn't conclusive. The accelerant was diesel, common for the yard. And even though it was a nonsmoking area, anyone could've sneaked a cigarette. So when a hundred thousand bucks shows up under the rug, Quinn decides to close the case without further thought."

"Let me guess. Janus wrote the check."

"Yep," Morgan said. "Janus didn't want the investigation of the dock fire to delay work on the *Sister*. He paid Quinn to keep quiet."

"This means we can look again at arson and put some resources behind it."

"Already done. Quinn speculates that the maximum amount of time it would take a cigarette to burn down and ignite the matches, setting off the diesel, would be approximately fifteen minutes. By then the concentration of propane in the tent would be enough for the explosion."

"Pretty simple."

"Yep," Morgan said. "I've got a warrant for the security guard's log. I'll question anybody who was still in the yard within a ten-to twenty-minute window of the fire."

Melika didn't respond.

"What?" Morgan asked.

"I'm just thinking. Harwood fits into that window, doesn't he?"

"We've been through this. He's got no motive."

"No. You're right. He doesn't."

There was a pause. She could hear Morgan flipping through his notes.

"Have you had a chance to check out Janus's cargo?" he asked.

"Not yet. I'm getting to know the cabin boy. I'm hoping he'll give me a tour of the holds. What about you? Were you able to figure out what's so damn important about this sand?"

"Maybe," Morgan said. "It's from one of Janus's abandoned quarries in Alaska."

"We knew that before I boarded."

"I dug a little deeper, no pun intended, and discovered that soon after his father died, Janus sent a mineralogist up to Alaska to see if any of the quarries had some life left."

"The rich always want more."

"Apparently he got lucky," Morgan said. "The mineralogist discovered a large vein of medium-grey sand. That indicates platinum was present. Normally, the concentration isn't high enough to refine."

"This one was?"

"I guess."

"Okay, but why ship it to England?" Melika asked.

"That I don't know yet. First thing in the morning, I'll call a geology professor at the university. A friend of mine."

"I wouldn't have guessed."

"That's it for me," he said. "What's new on your end?"

Melika sat back against the headboard. "Where do I start?"

"I heard about the guy waving from the funnel."

"That got everybody all excited." Mocking a creepy voice, she said, "A bad omen. O-o-o, scary."

"People aren't really buying that, are they?"

"A bad omen for the guy, that's for sure. He's dead."

"What happened?"

"I'm guessing he fell. Cracked his skull. I don't suspect foul play. Except it looks like someone tried to hide the body."

"Why?"

"Not sure," Melika said. "I didn't want anybody to know I'd been snooping around, so I sent a message to the captain anonymously. I wonder if we'll stop at Norfolk."

"Got a name?" Morgan asked.

"No. The only thing I found was a note in the guy's pocket. Hold on, I haven't taken time to look at it yet." Melika pulled the paper from her back pocket and flicked it open with one hand. "This figures," she said. "Janus's name and cabin number are scratched on it. Underneath, it says five thousand dollars."

"Sounds like another of Janus's payoffs."

"I think so."

"I'll check the missing persons reports," Morgan said. "But if he's traveling alone, no one may notice him gone until you're back in New York."

"Yeah, I was afraid of that."

"Okay. Anything else?"

She closed her eyes. "Yeah. Harwood. I'm dropping him as cover."

"You sure that's a good idea?"

"Look, I had to tell him we were using him."

"How'd he take it?"

She shrugged. "I don't know. Not well, I guess. He said I'd already blown it, my cover that is."

Morgan laughed. "I think you've met your match."

"What does that mean?"

"Melika, lighten up. You're going to burn out before you're forty."

"Burn out? Why don't you just butt out?"

"Without me, you wouldn't know what to do with yourself."

"Okay, okay." She took a deep breath and rubbed her eyes. "Anything else?"

Morgan yawned. "That's all I've got."

Melika hung up and settled back into the pillow. She checked her watch. One-fifteen in the morning. She should go to bed. She was tired. Not sleepy, though. The coffee had given her the jitters. She took a couple of deep breaths, trying to clear her head.

Her mind kept slipping back to Abram and his self-assured pronouncement that he was more of a threat than Janus. She wasn't scared of Abram. That was for sure. She wasn't scared of anybody, regardless of what Abram thought. But somewhere deep inside, Melika worried that his warning might be true.

She picked up her overnight case and set it on her lap. Apart from a small clutch stuffed with toiletries, it contained no personal items. Instead, it was nearly full of files regarding their investigation. She slipped funnel man's note into the file labeled "Evidence" and considered reorganizing the others. When she came across Abram's file, however, she closed the bag and turned on the TV. After five minutes of channel surfing, she gave up, opened the overnight case once more, skipped over Abram's file, and leafed through the others. She could always count on work to do. And she wanted to recheck the crew assignments anyway. Of course, it was at the bottom of the pile. Emptying the case, she noticed the book she'd thrown in as part of her last minute packing. It was *The Great Sea Disaster of the North Atlantic* from Abram's apartment. One of the many books he'd inherited from the yard superintendent, Blake Tellemann. At the back of the book were survivors' accounts of the sinking. Melika had wanted to read the story written by *Titanic*'s third-class passenger, Jakob Tellemann. It was no coincidence that he had the same last name as Blake. She had checked into it. Jakob was Blake's great-grandfather.

She tossed a blanket over her legs, fluffed up the pillows, and settled back.

Jakob Tellemann hooked her on the first line: "I was not a lucky man."

Why not? she wondered. He'd survived. Melika soon discovered that if you were a third-class passenger on *Titanic*, you had to count on your wits more than your luck. Evacuation was slow and disorganized. Jakob entrusted his young wife and infant son to a steward. He was the only member of the crew or staff leading people from third class to the boat deck. His orders: women and children *first*. Knowing time was running out, Jakob found his own escape route, but he reached the portside lifeboats only to discover that the rule was now women and children *only*. Undeterred, he checked the starboard side, and sure enough, men could have a seat if no women were around.

Jakob stepped inside the lifeboat and took his place, not realizing that lady luck had betrayed him. His wife and baby were not among the survivors. She'd refused to leave without him. With that knowledge haunting him every day, Jakob carried guilt heavier than the ship itself.

Melika dropped the book to her lap. "Jesus, does this shit ever end?"

Tragedy upon tragedy, the book was full of them. Innocent men, women, and children arraigned, tried, and sentenced to death in the anguishing two hours it took *Titanic* to sink. No appeals. No stay of execution. No consideration for cruel or unusual punishment. They were to drown in water colder than ice itself.

And for those who had escaped, they would be tortured for the rest of their lives by the heartache of losing a friend, lover, or family member in such a terrible way.

As Jakob Tellemann discovered, there was no luck that night. Everything was against them.

It was hard to imagine.

Melika marked the story with a piece of Algo stationary and flipped to the beginning of the book, where the circumstances surrounding the loss of *Titanic* were documented: its location when it hit the ice, the ice warnings received and ignored, the damage to the ship, and the numbers of those saved and lost. Facts. Things Melika could get her head around.

Out of the twenty-two hundred or more people aboard, Melika discovered that just over seven hundred survived.

She scanned the percentages of those saved by class. If there was any evidence of discrimination other than Jake Tellemann's testimony, it was in these numbers.

Sixty-two percent of the first-class passengers survived. Forty-two percent of those in second class got off the ship. Only twenty-five percent of third-class passengers lived to tell their story.

Melika scratched her chin. *What a waste of life.*

In the end, when all the lifeboats were gone, nearly seventy percent of *Titanic*'s passengers remained on the doomed ship. This was where any differential treatment ended. Regardless of class or race, those still aboard had to face and accept the same terrible and improvident fate.

Melika noticed something else in the book. She picked up a pencil from the nightstand and scratched down some numbers. To be fair, even though a smaller percentage of the third-class passengers survived, the number of people on board in third was double that of those in first. She saw a different picture when she ignored the percentages and looked only at the numbers saved in each group. Interesting. More of the crew survived than in any other class. What happened to going down with the ship? And there were almost as many saved in third class as there were in first. But in second class—the middle class—only a hundred or so lived, making them the least represented. *Some things never change. Wonder how the owners would've explained that?*

In the end, seventy-five percent of the women survived, along with fifty-two percent of the children, and only twenty percent of the men.

She snapped the book shut, realizing what she was doing—using numbers and statistics to distance herself from victims. *I'm a cop. I don't get close to anyone. It's safer that way. Cops and civilians don't mix.*

Driving her point home, Melika flicked her pencil across the room, a little vindictive move she stole from David Letterman, the late-night talk-show host. Except he took aim at the camera. Melika used the wall to represent the world she kept at arm's length.

Thinking that now she'd be able to sleep, she headed to the bathroom to brush her teeth and wash up.

As she dried her face, she studied her eyes in the mirror. Dark and sweet, like chocolate, her foster mom had always said.

Tossing the towel on the countertop, she took a step back from the sink. She looked at her body in profile, one side, and then the other, until she stood face-to-face with herself once again.

Abram's wrong. I'm not hiding behind my badge. Don't need to. I look good.

She couldn't shake the thought of Abram. She sighed. *Damn. I'm horny as hell.*

Chapter Eleven

For a second, Abram wasn't sure where he was. He could smell the salt air and hear the sound of waves breaking outside his window, but there wasn't the usual chorus of gulls squawking at the dawning light that greeted him at home. No, it was different here. Quiet, simple, and without that unavoidable sense of obligation that drew him from bed on a workday morning.

As the heaviness of a cognac-induced sleep lifted from his eyes, Abram untangled himself from the sheets and swung his legs over the edge of the bed. He sat there for a minute or two, reorienting himself to the layout of the cabin. The sunlight had not yet penetrated the window, but it had softened the darkness enough so he could distinguish the various pieces of furniture.

He stood, picked up his robe from the side chair, and headed to the window.

Outside, the ocean seemed endless, the blue surface sparkling as crests of lazy waves captured the first rays of the morning sun. Watching the reddish-yellow orb creep above the horizon, he thought about last night.

Melika had tried to dump him, suggesting he was little more than a cog in her investigative wheel. The excuse was a cop-out, pun intended. She wanted him as much as he wanted her.

From the time they'd first met at his apartment, when her blouse fell from her breasts, to dinner at Richard's, where she'd worn that sexy, head-turning outfit, she'd been leading him on. If she was simply playing hard to get, Abram wouldn't have given her another thought.

But last night, after seeing that look of fear pass across her face, he soon realized why Melika wouldn't go to bed with him. He didn't need to be a psychiatrist to see that she was scared of him. Or more accurately, she was scared of what she was beginning to feel for him. He knew she considered herself an independent, take-charge woman, needing no one. And for some reason, she vehemently resisted any emotion that endangered that image. She armored herself with her vocation and protected the façade at all costs.

So, in the heat of their argument, Abram had warned Melika to watch out for him. Because at some point he'd catch her off guard, get near enough to strip off that bulletproof vest she liked to wear, and make crazy wild love to her.

This morning, however, Abram wondered if the smart thing to do was simply walk away. Melika carried a hell of a lot of baggage in that head of hers. Maybe too much for even the strongest guy to handle.

Turning from the window, Abram pulled off his robe and decided he had to put her out of his mind.

Dressed in his jogging suit, he headed topside. A vigorous workout might do the trick.

Instead of entering the gymnasium, he walked aft, drawn to the rail by the steady sound of the ocean folding away from the *Sister*'s dark hull. The air, smelling faintly of salt, was clear and crisp, and a light layer of moisture sparkled on the open deck.

"Good morning."

Startled, Abram quickly glanced over his shoulder. It was the captain.

"Good morning," Abram responded, his breath turning white in the cool ocean air.

Captain Bartlett didn't smile. He nodded formally, as if the stillness of the morning would be broken by anything other than stoic respect. He stepped beside Abram, focusing on the water. Abram followed the captain's gaze.

For a few minutes they stood like brothers, one black, one white, silently speaking to each other about the beauty of the quiet ocean, the sun rising above it, and the defeat of so many who didn't respect it.

As Abram took a deep breath, pulling the cool air deep into his lungs, he caught the faint smell of an expensive cigar. Either the aroma triggered his imagination, or his mind was more powerful than he gave it credit. He saw and heard *Titanic* as surely as if he was on her.

Men in the smoking room below discussed the airplane, the automobile, and telephone as if each were little more than a passing fancy.

The gymnasium behind Abram came alive. The mechanical noise of bicycles, tread mills, and rowing machines from another era rattled through the arched windows.

From the promenade came the light and bouncy sound of giggling girls, the morning filled with the vitality of *Titanic* steaming at her greatest speed over the smooth and untroubled waters of the cold North Atlantic.

Ladies lounged on chaises and sipped tea, blankets folded neatly over their legs, the steward topping off their cups and offering each of them warm biscuits and jam. Strutting down the deck, young men, three or four in a group, laughed and jabbed each other in the ribs as pretty girls passed. And children, dressed in knickers, long socks, coats and caps, dodged the trouble-free adults strolling or milling about.

It was an age before world wars, terrorism, and global warming. A time of trust and satisfaction.

And it was alive on the *Sister*, as she too cut the sea at a fast, steady pace. On the vast ocean they traveled, not a vessel, not a plane in the sky, not even the stream from a jet, contradicted the impression of that simpler, calmer way of life.

Abram turned to the captain, but Bartlett had moved on. Or perhaps a contemporary officer didn't belong. Perhaps the past still had a hold on Abram, for as he approached the alcove to the gymnasium, he saw a man in a dark, old-fashioned uniform. He was tracing lines on the deck with a stick, perhaps a lifeguard's pole. The double row of brass buttons on his jacket, as well as the two shiny medals on his chest, caught the morning's soft light. Unmistakable on the sleeves of his uniform were the four gold bands indicating a captain's rank.

Abram stopped. "It's you," he said.

A bang echoed off the deckhouse. A crewman had come outside for a smoke, slamming the engineer's door. Seeing Abram, he raised his hand as if to say sorry.

Abram quickly looked back at the alcove. "Shit!" It was empty.

Darting from the rail, Abram hurried down the promenade to the gym. He opened the door, expecting to catch up with the man in the officer's uniform. The room was empty. He hustled back outside, bolted up the three steps across from the entry, and circled the raised roof over the first-class lounge.

No one except the crewman butting out his cigarette.

Abram yelled, "Did you see anyone? A guy in an old uniform carrying a long wooden pole?"

The crewman chuckled. "Nah, mac. Not since the circus left town."

"Smart ass," Abram muttered. He looked again down the length of the ship then retreated to the boat deck, rubbing his forehead.

At the bottom of the steps he froze.

Under his feet, in the sheltered area of the alcove, a message had been written in the fresh morning dew. A series of four numbers, two digits each, was quickly evaporating in the sun. Forty-two, twenty-five, forty-nine, and thirty. As Abram committed them to memory, an eerie sense of déjà vu struck him. He thought of Spin, who had given him different numbers at the shipyard fire, and he had no doubt that the man he'd just seen was another of the three trespassers who had interrupted his search for Blake at the launch.

Abram leaned against the deckhouse wall and rubbed his neck. *Who were these guys, and why were they taunting him?* He closed his eyes to think. Maybe it wasn't just him. Maybe it was another of Janus's attempts to lend realism to his ship. Maybe he had actors wandering the decks like ghosts. That was plausible, knowing Janus.

But as Abram ran his foot over the spot where the latest message had been, he remembered what had transpired after the fire. No one had believed him. Apparently, the man who'd given Abram the first message didn't exist.

Still, there had to be a logical explanation.

Foregoing his workout, Abram returned to his cabin and jotted down the two messages on a piece of stationary. It was White Star stationary, he noticed. Not Algo's, Janus's company.

Abram sat at the desk, staring at the paper, hoping to make sense of the two sets of numbers. He turned when he heard a knock at the door adjoining his father's cabin.

"Want some breakfast?" Clay asked.

Abram placed the paper on the desk. "Yeah, I could use something," he said, taking another look at the numbers before setting down his pen. He leaned back in the chair. "Pop, can I ask you something?"

"Shoot." He sat on the edge of the bed.

"Have you ever thought you were going crazy?"

"Sure."

"I don't mean the everyday pull-your-hair-out kind of crazy. I mean the seeing-things-that-don't-exist type."

Clay raised his eyebrows.

"Come on, Pop," Abram said. "You must think there's some truth to these otherworldly things, or you wouldn't be wearing that amulet around your neck."

"I told you," Clay said, pulling it out from under his shirt and rubbing it with his thumb. "I like the way it looks, that's all."

"I know better than that."

"Okay, okay." Clay tucked it back under his shirt. "I don't understand a lot of things. Doesn't mean I don't believe in them."

Abram sat forward, elbows on his legs. "Like what?"

"I don't know." Clay ran his hand over his head. "Like I'm certain I'll be reunited with my family after I die."

"Then you believe in spirits. Ghosts."

"I have no reason not to."

Abram took a heavy breath, glancing at the piece of paper with the messages.

Clay crossed his arms. "What's this about, son?"

"If I knew," Abram said, "you'd be the first to know."

"Let me tell you a secret," Clay said, "that might ease your mind some. But keep it to yourself, okay?" He looked around as if eavesdroppers had moved in close. "Your mother made me promise not to tell anyone. Especially you."

"Okay."

"When you were just hours old ..."

Abram made a sour face. He hated these how-cute-you-were stories.

"Hear me out," Clay said. "Your mother was cradling you in her arms. It was dark, but she was sure she saw something at the end of her hospital bed. Not a nurse. Or a doctor. She said it was something familiar, yet something she couldn't describe. She wasn't scared. In fact, she could feel warmth from it and a sense of peace that stayed with her even as she watched it disappear. She thought it was a sign. That you were different. Special."

"And you believed her?"

Clay sat up defiantly. "Of course I did," he said.

Abram was surprised. Since the divorce, Pop seldom defended Mom.

Clay settled back. "You know your mother," he said, returning to his off-handed manner. "She's pushy and overbearing. But she's not crazy. And neither are you."

"I hope not," Abram said.

"You gotta trust yourself, son. Or you *will* go nuts." He slapped his knees and stood. "Come on. Let's get breakfast."

Chapter Twelve

Abram and Clay decided to check out the Parisian Cafe on B deck for breakfast.

The maitre d' escorted them to a table by the window, and Abram studied the unique room.

It was long and narrow yet had an open, airy feel with its light-colored walls and white wicker furniture. The ship's large windows ran the length of one wall. Fake windows—though it was tough to tell—lined the opposite wall. Artificially lit from behind, they created the warmth of a late afternoon sun regardless of the time of day. Latticework decorated the remainder of the room, and real ivy climbed the rungs. On the next cruise, Abram thought, these vigorous plants would be spreading across the ceiling.

For an hour, Abram and Clay lingered over breakfast, watching the ocean pass endlessly below them.

The waitress had just refreshed their coffees when Clay brought up Melika.

"Is she not going to meet up with us this morning?" he asked.

"I doubt it," Abram said, picking up the sugar.

"Trouble already?"

"Yep." He sweetened his coffee more than usual because, what the heck, he was on vacation.

"I'm not surprised. She's a handful. Stubborn." Clay shrugged. "Like your mother."

"No, she's not." Abram set the sugar bowl heavily on the table.

"Are you sure this isn't about losing? You've always been tenacious, getting what you set your mind to."

"Melika's the same."

"I've noticed."

Abram stood and pushed his chair away. "Let's get some air. I'll show you around a little bit."

They walked toward the bow, the deck filling with people taking in the morning.

"It sure is crowded around the lifeboats," Clay said, moving aside to let a couple pass.

Abram glanced down the deck at the array of little crafts. "In *Titanic*'s day, only one lifeboat per station was required. Not nearly enough for all the passengers and crew."

"Hopefully that oversight has been corrected."

Abram nodded. "On the *Sister*, each station has three lifeboats. See?"

The boats sat in a half-pyramid pattern, the one closest to the edge of the ship mounted on deck, the remaining two hanging above. Janus couldn't buy or weasel his way around it. All vessels required enough lifeboats to accommodate everyone aboard. Because of *Titanic*. The significant loss of her passengers had resulted in the change of regulation.

Still, Abram thought, the number of lifeboats on the *Sister* did look like overkill.

"Must take forever to get them all launched," Clay said, glancing at the huge davits that swung each boat over the side.

"Not really. They're fully automated. And failsafe." Abram reached up and knocked on the hull of the third lifeboat overhead. It was fiberglass, painted to look like wood.

"Give me good old-fashioned brains and brawn over all that computer stuff," Clay said, and they continued their walk.

A child ran past, taking advantage of the opportunity to get ahead of her parents. Abram and Clay stepped aside for mom and dad to give chase.

That's when Abram discovered the subtle difference between the second and third boats and the ones mounted on deck below them. It was creepy. There was no other word for it.

The name stenciled on the top two boats was *Titan's Sister*. That was the way it should be. The other boat, the one secured to the deck, was marked *Titanic*.

As they passed each station, Abram confirmed the same markings. There was nothing to do except laugh it off. Janus's games. It really did appear he'd thought of everything.

Fortunately, his father hadn't noticed the markings.

Near the aft section of the deck, Clay turned and took the three steps up to a platform over the raised roof of the smoking room.

"Thought we could sit a minute," he said. He picked a bench facing the storage closets and the fourth funnel.

Pop surveyed the deckhouses around him. "You did a nice job, Abram."

Abram chuckled. His father's seal of approval, delivered without fanfare, was typically delayed by quiet scrutiny. It was valued nonetheless.

"I had a good team of welders," Abram said.

"You headed up the team."

"True." Abram raised his head to admire the structures around them. "This deck was the greatest challenge."

"Quite a change from the long runs of plating inside the ship, I'd imagine."

"I'll admit, it took a lot of finesse to make it look like *Titanic*. And you know what it's like to work with aluminum."

Clay nodded. "Tough to get a clean cut unless you're using propane. I think you managed fine. Look how fast you got the promenade deck enclosed."

Abram rubbed his knees with the palm of his hands.

"Uh-oh," Clay said.

"What?"

Melika was climbing the steps to the raised roof.

Clay got to his feet. "Gotta go," he said. "Wanna get some souvenirs at the mall."

Melika and Pop exchanged hellos as they passed.

With her hands in her pants pockets and her back straight, Melika walked in Abram's direction, pacing herself.

Abram stood.

Several yards away, she stopped.

Not knowing what else to do, Abram gestured to the bench. They sat, Melika at one end, Abram at the other.

She looked around. "Nice day."

"Yeah."

"Sea's calm."

"Uh-huh."

She glanced in his direction. "A little cool, though."

"Supposed to warm up some, I guess."

Melika nodded, perhaps uncomfortable with the early lull in the conversation. Abram didn't know what to say. It seemed she'd calmed down after last night, but he doubted she wanted to apologize.

"Look," she said. "About last night."

Abram rubbed his eye. He wasn't up for this discussion. He'd rather go back to bed. Alone. Hopefully he'd wake up refreshed, without the early twentieth century and its obscure men, cryptic messages, and *Titanic* lifeboats rattling around his brain. "Forget it," he told Melika. "I understand."

"I don't," she said. "I mean, I'm not sure."

Abram looked up, surprised. "What do you mean, you're not sure?"

"You said I should be watching *you*, not Janus."

"Oh, that."

"I know I was blunt," Melika said. "A little abrasive. You gotta understand. That's my style. It comes from playing the bad cop, making suspects talk."

"Suspects? You still consider me a suspect?"

"I want you to understand," she said. "It's important to me—to my work—to not get wrapped up in stuff insignificant to the case. Not get too close to things."

"People, you mean."

"What?"

"Not get too close to *people*."

"Don't patronize me," she said.

"Melika, I'm not trying to be antagonistic. That's your area of expertise."

"Let's not sling any more mud. All right?"

"Are you trying to apologize?"

"Of course not. I'm trying to explain."

"Why?"

It was obvious she didn't know; her mouth opened partway but no words came out. Finally: "It's nothing personal."

Abram studied her closely, looking deeply into her eyes. "That's not true," he said. "Not the bad cop stuff. Not the distancing yourself for the benefit of your career. You're kidding yourself, Melika. It's *very* personal."

"No. Damn it." She balled her hands into tight fists. "You have no idea what it's like. Every day I see the terrible things people do to each other. Savage, brutal stuff. You gotta understand. Bodies gutted, burned ..." She caught her breath, realizing how loud and coarse she'd become.

A passing jogger, trying to cheat on a lap by cutting across the raised roof, heard Melika. He immediately stopped, turned, and hustled back down the stairs with his head down.

Her teeth clenched and voice controlled, Melika said, "If you were me, you'd figure out a way to desensitize yourself and keep things—*people*—at arm's length, too."

Abram envied the jogger. Cut and run. Don't look back.

He put his hand on Melika's knee with enough pressure to stop it from jiggling up and down. "Here's what I think," he said. "Criminals, you can handle. Mutilated bodies? Sure, you've figured out a way to cope. But me? I scare the shit out of you. And you have no idea what to do about it."

He expected a quick, combative response. But she just stared at him. Perhaps she was trying to decide whether to go with a right hook or a left uppercut. Abram was prepared to protect himself from both. What he wasn't prepared for was how her expression started to change. A look of surrender, though subtle, crept into her eyes. The muscles in her face loosened, making her look older, more mature, weaker, yet far more attractive—if that was the least bit possible.

"What do you want from me, Abram? A pound of my flesh?"

"That would be the heart," he said.

"So I've been told."

"I'm not the bad guy."

"No?" she said. "Then why does it seem like it's been one thing after another ever since we met?"

"How so?"

She breathed out, quick and short. "My investigations. They used to be straightforward. I knew what action to take. Decisions were simple."

"Now they're not?"

"Right."

"And that involves me because?"

"Because ..." She wasn't prepared to answer. "Take that picture you've got hanging in your apartment," she said.

"Picture? You mean the photo of *Titanic*'s memorials?"

"Yeah. Remember? It was a few days after the fire, the first time we talked. I went to your place to apologize for Morgan's interrogation techniques."

"I thought you were sizing up my apartment."

"Yeah, that, too," she said. "Anyway, normally I wouldn't notice such things. But you know what I thought? I thought, what kind of a person hangs a picture so macabre?"

"Did you figure it out?"

"The problem was that *I* found it intriguing. At the time, it seemed simple. For one thing, it was a black and white print. Black and white in a figurative sense, too. I mean, what could be more basic—more straightforward—than a cemetery? Just stones and earth. That's what I thought you were trying to convey by not shooting it in color."

Abram shook his head. "Nothing is that simple."

"That's what sca—" The word Abram was looking for was just about out of her mouth. He wanted her to say it. To admit to it. She didn't. "That's what bothers me," she corrected herself. "I can't get it out of my mind. It's haunting me."

"Haunting you?" Abram didn't like the choice of words.

"A figure of speech."

"Right."

"What is it, then? What is it in that black and white photo that I'm not seeing?"

"Gray," he said.

"Fuck off!"

"I'm not trying to be a smart-ass."

"Then answer my question."

"Okay ... well ... gray areas are like shadows. Areas of uncertainty. Doubt. Mistrust. Naturally, one would feel vulnerable, sca—" He cleared his throat, playing with the fact that she'd dodged the word earlier. "Naturally, one would feel scared," he said.

She narrowed her eyes, not amused.

Abram shook his head. Such a tough, intelligent woman, yet so unaware of the extraordinary adventures open to someone willing to take risks, to make compromises, to meet people halfway. "You know what you're missing out on?" he said, flatly. "Life. Life's what you choose to ignore."

"Life?"

"Remember what we talked about that day in my apartment? Not just the picture and *Titanic*'s foundering, but the senselessness of all tragic events?"

"And the gut-wrenching questions that result for those left behind."

"Yeah," Abram said. "You understood in a way someone without that experience would not. It led me to believe that you too had suffered something tragic at some point in your past."

Melika looked away.

Abram said, "I'm guessing that's where you lost touch with it. Distanced yourself from it. Life, I mean."

She said nothing.

"When you were a kid, maybe?"

"It was nothing. Years ago."

In an expression she struggled to keep indifferent, Abram saw the telltale signs of anger and resentment. "You lost someone close to you," he said.

She nodded. "My parents. And older brother."

"How?"

"Plane crash. A commuter from Birmingham to Atlanta."

"I remember something about that," Abram said. "Faulty wiring."

"Mice chewed through the insulation." She chuckled sadly. "Remarkable really. Something so small taking down something a million times its size."

Abram nodded.

"It's not like the airline didn't know about it," she said. "Maintenance reported mice at least a month earlier. But they never grounded the plane. Just happened that the deadly flight was the one my family was on."

"That's a tough one."

Something in Melika's expression changed, some other emotion pushing anger and resentment aside. "It was my fault," she said.

There it was. Guilt. Abram should've recognized it. "No," he said, certain Melika wasn't to blame. He also understood that whatever the circumstances were, guilt was not an easy burden to unload. What could he do other than make the standard statement in no uncertain terms? "It was not your fault."

She stared deep into his eyes, a rather sobering look. "You don't understand. They were on their way to a wedding. I wanted to go, but I was too young. I made such a fuss that they missed their flight. They took the next one. The one that crashed."

"Jesus, Melika."

She offered nothing more. Abram sat quiet, too.

After a moment, Melika took a deep breath and stood. "My problem. Not yours," she said.

Abram stood, too. "Okay," he replied. What else could he say?

Taking a step toward the stairs, she looked back at him, pointing at his feet. "Love the shoes, by the way."

"My shoes?" He looked down. One was brown. One was black. "Shit."

"Change into some runners," she said. "Meet me at the squash courts. Twelve sharp. I'll beat your butt."

"Two to one you don't."

Her smile was sly. "I'll take that bet."

Chapter Thirteen

"What took you so long to call?"

"Morgan, calm down." Melika was sitting on the edge of her bed, cradling the phone on her shoulder while she massaged her feet with her hands. It took nearly two hours and her whole body would be sore tomorrow, but she'd finally beaten Harwood in three out of four squash games. It had let off some steam. Like a relief valve. She felt more like herself.

"I've got news," Morgan said.

"Good or bad?"

"I'll let you judge."

"Okay, go."

"I checked out the security guard's log on the day of the fire," Morgan said. "Most of the workers had left for lunch so there were only nine people at the dock just before the fire started. I've talked to all of them. Dan Johnson's our arsonist."

"Dan Johnson," Melika said. "Never heard of him."

"He's a maintenance man. Low seniority and a sympathizer with the group picketing the yard."

"Figures. Why's it always the obvious that comes back to bite us in the ass?"

"It might be more interesting than you think. While I had the log, I figured why not. I'll look up the entries on the day of the launch."

"And?"

"Janus signed in just three minutes after Blake Tellemann. Apart from security, they were the only two in the yard for nearly an hour."

"That *is* interesting." Melika propped herself up on her elbows.

"I want to know what Janus was doing for that hour."

"I'll see what I can find out. I've arranged to have dinner with him tonight at the captain's table. I might get something out of that."

"Are you taking Harwood?"

"Just following orders. What else you got?" she asked.

Melika could hear Morgan shuffling papers. "Okay," he said. "I talked to my engineering friend about the platinum sand."

"Good. What's up?"

"Now, follow me on this. Platinum is typically alloyed with a mineral called osmium. One of the by-products of refining platinum from the osmium is something called tetroxide. It's toxic. But easy to neutralize."

Melika yawned. "So?"

"Try to stay awake. This is good."

"Okay."

"Remember Janus's mineralogist?"

She closed her eyes, thinking back. "The guy who discovered the sand in one of Janus's Alaskan quarries?"

"Yeah. He figures there's nearly five hundred million bucks of platinum in the *Sister* alone. With probably three times that sitting in the quarry."

"Holy shit!"

"That's an understatement. But there's a problem."

She shrugged. "Always."

"Janus's platinum isn't alloyed with pure osmium. It can be refined, but the mineralogist thinks there may be issues neutralizing the by-product."

"What kind of issues?"

"Toxic issues."

"Oh. That's not good." She stretched, pulling kinks out of her neck. "Wait a minute." She froze. "Does that mean I'm sitting on half a billion dollars of hazardous material?"

"Take it easy. It's completely inert in its natural state."

"You sure?"

"It sat in Alaska for the last hundred million years or so. I'm guessing it'll be fine in the *Sister*'s hold for the next few days."

"That's not funny. This ship is creepy enough as it is. So, what happens to the sand in England?"

"It looks like it's headed for a company called ..." He shuffled papers again. "Here it is ... Stone Industries."

"A refining company?"

"Yep."

"Why all the secrecy?" Melika fluffed some pillows, settling back again.

"If news gets out about the discovery, the bottom will fall out of the precious metals market."

"Big deal. His five hundred million drops to a hundred million. It'd still be enough for me."

"Plus, there's always the danger of piracy."

"True enough."

"At least now we know why Janus is in such a rush to keep *Titan's Sister* on schedule," Morgan said.

"Maybe that's what this boat is all about. A cargo ship might draw attention. But who would think a cruise ship would be carrying anything except luggage?"

"The deck plan of the holds supports that theory. That reminds me. Is funnel man still on ice?"

"I guess so," Melika said. "Did you figure out who he was?"

"Several men are traveling alone. Who knows which one, if any, is your guy. No missing person's report has been filed."

"All right. Anything else?"

"Nope. What about you?"

"No." She checked the time. "I'd better go. I'm meeting Michael in ten minutes, then I've gotta run down to Scotland Row and find something to wear to the captain's table."

"Who's Michael?"

"The cabin boy I told you about. He stole a passkey for the holds so I can check out the sand. The kid's a regular Mini Me." She reached for her pocket book. "Hey, Morgan," she said, picking out a credit card that wasn't near its limit. "Do you think I can expense a new outfit?"

She heard his chair squeak. She pictured him leaning back, his feet on the desk, a smug look on his face. "As long as you don't go overboard," he said.

"Funny, Morgan. Very funny."

Chapter Fourteen

Abram snagged two snails in puff pastry from the waitress meandering through the restaurant's reception area. The hors d'oeuvre was a little chewy, he decided, and he offered Melika the one he had left. She was on her toes, scanning the room, rubbing her hand up and down the paper baton she'd made by rolling up their dinner invitations.

"Where's that maitre d'?" she asked of no one in particular.

Abram shrugged and popped the remaining snail in his mouth.

"I think I see him," she said, falling back on her heels.

The maitre d', a short, stiff-looking man, moved quickly through the crowd. "The captain has been detained," he said when he reached Melika and Abram.

"Nothing serious, I hope," Melika said.

"Ship's business," the maitre d' replied, preoccupied with his guest list. He checked off Melika and Abram. "If you'll follow me, I'll show you to your table."

Melika stayed on the maitre d's coattails. Abram hadn't intended to lag behind, but a pushy couple cut in front of him. It was fortuitous because, at a distance, he got a good look at the back of Melika's dress. Very revealing. Shoulders exposed, low cut, nothing except the tight fit of the material keeping the garment in place.

As for his own attire, Abram had rented one of the most expensive tuxes in the ship's haberdashery. No tails, no frills. Just a simple, stylish look that made him feel like a million bucks.

He tugged at his vest, making sure it was straight, then took his seat at the captain's table.

It wasn't long before Mr. and Mrs. Abe Strauss, an elderly couple celebrating their fiftieth wedding anniversary, joined Abram and Melika. John and Judy Aston were next. They looked to be in their early fifties and well off. Old money, Abram decided, because they both appeared keen and carefree, no wrinkles or shakes from the burden of daily stress.

Abram moved closer to the table, settling in. The chair, with its broad, stiff back and leather-trimmed arms, was surprisingly comfortable.

He picked up a knife, noting it was silver, not stainless, but quickly replaced it when he saw Janus and the captain approaching their table.

"Heads up," he whispered to Melika. "Captain's coming."

Janus was the first to greet the guests. "Good evening," he said. "I'm Bruce Janus, the owner of Algo Cruise Lines."

He touched the captain's arm lightly. "May I introduce our commander, Captain Timothy Bartlett."

Bartlett was no more than forty or forty-five, disciplined and reserved, his hair, beard, and mustache completely black. He greeted his guests with a business-like composure.

Janus, however, had never cultivated an authoritative, professional demeanor, even though he'd inherited a billion-dollar company. With his cropped hair and thin mustache, he looked young. Nor did his voice have an assertive tenor. Although it was lively and upbeat, it often sounded fake and childlike.

"Good to see you again," Janus said to Abram.

Abram nodded.

As soon as the captain sat, Melika grabbed his attention. "So," she said, "what was the problem?"

"Ma'am?" he asked.

Abram tried to contain a smirk. The captain had already blown it. Melika hated it when someone called her "ma'am."

She crossed her arms. "The maitre d' said you were detained on the bridge."

"Yes. I apologize for that." Bartlett adjusted his chair, centering himself in front of his place. "Our ship-to-shore radio has a minor problem."

"Certainly nothing to worry about," Janus said, looking eagerly around the table. "How is everyone enjoying the cruise?"

Along with the other guests at the table, Abram said it was great, although Judy Aston was eager to break up the idle chit-chat. "Excuse me, captain," she said. Her voice was strong, like Melika's.

"Yes."

"You mentioned your ship-to-shore radio. Didn't *Titanic* have a radio problem as well?"

Bartlett took a sip of water. "Ma'am, I wouldn't know."

Judy's husband chimed in. "You'll have to forgive my wife," he said. "After we booked this cruise, she became a *Titanic* fanatic."

Judy hit John playfully on the arm. "Stop calling me that." She turned to Janus. "You'd know. *Titanic* had radio problems, didn't she?"

Janus pulled the linen serviette from his wine glass. "Yes, she did," he said, draping it over his lap. "*Titanic*'s Marconi operators worked tirelessly for hours, hoping to repair the radio. Luckily, they got it working before they hit the iceberg."

"Otherwise," Judy said, "no one would've known *Titanic* sank."

"Until it didn't show up at port," Melika replied.

"That would've been days later," Judy said. "Too late for anyone freezing in a lifeboat." She shook her head. "Amazing how much we take for granted nowadays."

"It's true." Janus motioned to the sommelier, a tall, young woman who opened a bottle of Bordeaux. "Communication methods are far more sophisticated than they used to be. In fact, *Titan's Sister* can automatically and continually call for assistance, switching to back-up and redundant systems if need be."

"Oh, I wasn't worried," Judy said. "No, no."

The captain picked up his wine glass. "Please, join me," he said, "in congratulating Mr. and Mrs. Strauss on their fiftieth wedding anniversary."

They were a quiet, humble couple, Mr. Strauss thanking their host softly.

Janus proposed a second toast to celebrate a successful voyage to date. After a slight pause, he lifted his glass a little higher. "To fine, clear seas ahead."

"Clear seas ahead," Judy said like an old seaman.

All those at the table took a sip of wine then leaned back as the waiter ladled soup into their bowls.

While everyone tasted what looked like cream of leek, Melika pushed hers aside and once again addressed Bartlett. "So, captain. Tell me. If you strip off the *Titanic* guise, how does the *Sister* compare to other ships?"

After a pause, he said, "It's a very advanced ship."

"What do you think?" Judy asked. "Do you think *Titanic*'s fatal flaw was man or machine?"

"Too many ifs," Janus said, peppering his soup. "If the look-outs had had binoculars, if they'd hit the iceberg dead on instead of glancing off it, if one bulkhead had gone a deck higher—"

"Don't forget about the human factor," Judy said. "The ice warnings, the speed of the ship. Were her officers too confident in a vessel labeled practicably unsinkable?"

"Captain, let's hear from you." It was Melika.

"Yes, yes," Judy said.

Bartlett cleared his throat. "On the sea, the captain relies on nothing but his own judgment."

Judy again. "So you don't think Captain Smith, on his last voyage before retirement, was complacent?"

Bartlett shook his head. "Smith commanded the largest vessel in the world. One doesn't attain that honor without sound judgment."

"Then how the hell did it sink?" Melika blurted out. "Sorry," she said, lowering her voice.

"Like I said," Janus answered. "It was all those ifs. Had one thing been different—"

"Let's hear from you, Mr. Harwood." Bartlett's voice easily overpowered Janus's.

"Me?" Abram had been happily eating his soup.

"You built the *Sister*, did you not?" Bartlett asked.

"Well, not exactly. I headed up the welding teams."

"Really?" Judy turned to Abram. "Then you must have an opinion on why *Titanic* sank."

Abram leaned back, allowing the waitress to remove his soup bowl and serve the apple-walnut watercress salad.

He picked up his fork. "Umm." He poked at some walnuts and a couple pieces of apple, unsure what to say. Janus was right. Like so many tragedies, the reason never came down to a single cause. Abram thought of Blake. How true it was regarding his death. Clearing his throat, Abram said, "I know how compelling it is ... to find something or someone to blame. In *Titanic*'s case, so many things were against her that not even 20/20 hindsight makes it possible."

Janus and Judy were nodding.

Melika took hold of the conversation again. She looked at the captain. "I hear that most cruise ships are not much more than a hotel on a barge."

"That's true," he said.

"But not this one. How does it handle?"

"Very well."

Janus said, "With side thrusters and enhanced stabilizers, she can outmaneuver anything on the water."

Melika turned her head toward Janus but kept her eyes on the captain. "Is that with or without cargo in the bow?"

The captain's eyes narrowed slightly. "The ship automatically adjusts to varying loads."

Janus interrupted. "I don't really think our guests are interested in that." He turned to the couple on his left. "Mr. and Mrs. Strauss. You've barely said a word."

Melika wasn't going to give them the chance. She said to Janus, "Okay. Tell me about Scotland Row."

"What about it?"

"You've been so careful with details. You have Turkish baths, electric baths, even a darkroom. Everything as it was in 1912. Except E deck. It's a mall. *Titanic* never had a mall."

"You're right, she didn't."

"So what, then? Is the commercial aspect of this ship more important than authenticity?"

"Of course she has to pay for herself," Janus said.

Judy decided it was her turn to press Janus. "I've wondered about that, too," she said. "I've shopped on the Row, of course. Wonderful things. But I wanted to see how it was in 1912."

Janus held his response until the waiter removed the warming cover from his dinner. He rotated his plate so the vegetables were at the front, his roast beef and Yorkshire pudding at the back. "The Row," he said, inspecting his fork, turning it slightly as if it were a mirror, "is where the third-class families gathered, hoping for direction, feeling lost and forgotten in the bowels of the sinking ship." Apparently, Janus didn't like what he saw when looking at the fork. He passed it to the waiter who quickly gave him another one.

Armed with his silverware, he looked Judy straight in the eye. "If there are such things as troubled spirits, Ms. Aston, no doubt they'd be found on Scotland Row."

Judy sat back. "Oh, I see."

Abram stopped chewing.

"Whoa, wait a minute." Melika pointed her fork at Janus. "Using that logic, you never should've built the ship in the first place. Every deck had more than its share of tragedies."

"But I *had* to build this ship," Janus said flatly.

"Why?"

He smiled. "I'm a *Titanic* fanatic." He touched Judy's hand.

"Thank you," she said with a proud smile.

"You're welcome." He fluffed up his napkin. "Now, let's eat."

Except for the occasional remark about the tenderness of the meat or the seasoning of the potatoes, the table was quiet while everyone finished the main course.

Abram occasionally glanced at Janus and the captain. A strange kind of energy seemed to pass between the three of them, as if they knew more about each other than they were willing to understand.

After dessert of rice custard pudding and fruit flan, Mr. and Mrs. Strauss explained they were getting tired and excused themselves. The waiter approached the table, cleared the vacated spots, and whisked the crumbs away. A waitress offered coffee. Judy and John declined. They were off for a cigarette, they explained, though Abram didn't figure them for tobacco smokers. He figured pot was more their style.

"Ms. Jones," Bartlett said, studying Melika over the rim of his coffee cup. "I understand you are a police officer. A detective." His tone sounded more investigative than social. Was the captain playing detective himself?

She hesitated, and it paid off.

A man dressed in a dark blue suit, too plain for a passenger, approached the table and leaned between the captain and Janus.

The conversation was brief, Bartlett dismissing the man quickly.

Melika said, "That was Randy Fae, wasn't it? Head of ship's security?"

Bartlett pushed back his chair and stood. "Yes." He looked at his watch. "Well, I must get back to the bridge."

Janus trailed after him, leaving Abram and Melika alone.

"Nuts?" Abram asked.

"Huh?"

"Nuts? Cheese?"

The waiter had dropped off an assortment.

She took a quick look at the plate and picked up a piece of Havarti. Taking one bite, she chewed it slowly, watching Janus and the captain weave through the tables to the door.

Abram liked the look of the white cheddar. "Do you believe in that stuff about haunted decks?" he asked.

"Of course not," she said without hesitation.

Abram helped himself to the nuts. With a loose fist, he shook them in his hand as if rolling dice at a crap game. Maybe he should get Melika to blow on them for luck.

That wasn't going to happen.

Abruptly, she stood, tossed her napkin on the table, and headed after Janus. Over her shoulder, she said, "I'll be right back."

Abram had heard that one before.

* * * *

Melika moved quickly through the restaurant, catching up with Janus and the captain near the elevator. Neither looked happy to see her.

"Mr. Janus," she said. "I forgot to ask you about the enclosed promenade. Was it part of the 1912 design?"

"The promenade?" Janus never passed up an opportunity to talk about his ship. He turned to the captain and said, "We can talk later."

The elevator chimed, and the captain glanced at Melika with an unmistakable I'm-watching-you look before he slipped through the closing doors.

"You're sure proud of this boat," Melika said when she and Janus were alone.

"Ship," he corrected her.

"What?"

"It's a ship. Not a boat." He brushed the front of his jacket and picked off a piece of lint. "Now," he said, "you were asking about the promenade."

"Actually, now that we're alone, I'm more interested in empty propane tanks and half-burned cigarettes."

Janus narrowed his eyes. "What are you talking about?"

"We know about your deal with Fire Marshall Quinn."

"Quinn? I don't know anyone by that name." He turned toward the elevator.

Melika grabbed his arm. "Sure you do," she said. "You bribed him to close the investigation on the dock fire."

Janus pulled free and shrugged to straighten his jacket. "That's ridiculous."

"Is it? Quinn says different."

"Pfft," he said, waving her off. "Quinn's an idiot. It's his word against mine."

Melika didn't skip a beat. "Your word might not mean much after what happened to funnel man."

"Who?"

"Play dumb all you want. I found the body in the ventilation room. He was carrying a slip of paper with your name on it."

An older couple moved slowly toward the elevator, the man relying heavily on a cane, his wife supporting him with both her hands tucked under his elbow. Before shuffling away, they smiled at Melika and Janus, Janus engaging them with a host-like demeanor that rivaled Martha Stewart's.

He didn't have the same regard for Melika. "I didn't kill him," Janus said quietly, "if that's what you're getting at."

"Maybe not. But you failed to notify the family and that, my friend, is enough to get this ship turned around in a heart beat."

"No, it isn't," he said. "First, funnel man, as you like to call him, has no family. I pulled him off the street. Second, I intend to see he gets a proper burial when we get back. Unless," he said, holding up his finger as if he just had a good idea, "you could talk the captain into a service at sea."

Two kids raced up to Janus, wanting his autograph on a souvenir postcard. The father stood apologetically a few steps back while Janus leaned down, told the children how happy he was to have them on board, and slowly inscribed their postcards according to their exacting instructions. Still smiling, Janus waved to the children as they hurried off to their next adventure.

"Anything else?" he said to Melika.

"Anything else? I'm just getting started."

Noticing a group of stewards, Janus held up his hand to get their attention. "You're doing a wonderful job," he said to them. "Tell all the cabin staff, I'm very pleased."

"Janus, the longer you screw around, the longer this is going to take."

He turned abruptly to Melika, looking irritated. "What are you doing on my ship anyway?"

She backed off, but only a little. "Just keeping Abram company."

"Pfft. I know Harwood. You're not his type."

"And what type is that?" *Who is he to judge? He's smirking, the son-of-a-bitch. He thinks he's gotten me off topic.*

She continued, "You've gone out of your way to keep your boat—"

"Uh-uh—" he raised his forefinger.

"To keep your *ship* on schedule. I think I know why, and I doubt you're smart enough to pull it off."

His eyes widened; his mouth fell.

It was her turn to smirk.

Crossing his arms, he said, "Look, let me explain the business world to you. It's standard practice to cut through red tape, cut corners."

"Standard business practice, huh? Is it standard business practice to load cargo in the dead of night?"

"Yes, as a matter of fact."

"And not list it on the manifest?"

"An oversight." He turned to call the elevator.

Melika stretched her arm in front of him, blocking him. Little more than a foot was between them. "You know what else I discovered?"

"I can only imagine."

"I know about your little rendezvous with Tellemann. Remember? The morning of the ship's launch?" Her fishing paid off. Janus, the man who could scowl at her one minute then turn and charm the passengers the next, looked serious and wary.

Melika said, "The morning of the launch, you and Tellemann were alone in the shipyard for nearly an hour."

"Tellemann's death was an accident," Janus said quickly, strongly. "The coroner had no doubts."

"Right. An accident," she said. "That's what you want everyone to believe."

"It *was* an accident."

"No, see, you found out that Tellemann didn't want to go ahead with the launch. You followed him into the yard, determined to convince him otherwise. When you didn't get your way, you blindsided him with a two by four. Set it up to look like an accident. That's murder, my friend. Big time."

"No, it wasn't like that."

"No? Then what *was* it like?"

He glanced over one shoulder then the other. He lowered his voice. "Look, Tellemann was already dead when I found him. At least I thought he was."

"You found him? And you didn't tell anybody. Abram was searching all over the place."

"There was no time. I was going to report it after the launch."

She grabbed his shoulder and pinned him to the wall so they were face-to-face. "Jesus, Janus! If you'd told somebody, Tellemann might still be alive."

"You don't think I've thought of that?" He tried to push her arm away. "But it was his fault."

"How?"

"Do you know why Tellemann wanted to cancel the launch?"

Melika shook her head.

"He had a gut feeling. *A gut feeling.*"

"So?"

He looked at her as if she were the most thick-headed person on earth. "Cancel the launch because of a gut feeling? That's ridiculous. The morning was perfect."

Melika backed off a little. "But Tellemann was right, wasn't he? The ship nearly broke in two."

Janus didn't answer.

Melika continued. "Look, I'd like to help you out here. The way it looks, your failure to act resulted in Tellemann's death. If the district attorney gets wind of it, he'll charge you with reckless endangerment. That's a felony. Jail time. And I don't think you'd do well in the slammer."

Janus took a deep breath and shook his head. "What is it you want?" He sounded more annoyed than threatened.

"What have you got in the holds, Janus?"

"How do you know about that?"

"I'm smart."

Playing on his ego didn't work this time. "It's none of your damn business," he said.

She tried threatening him. "It is if it's a prohibited substance. Toxic."

"Toxic? Pfft."

"Contraband. Drugs."

"I've told you enough. Besides, you can't do anything about it. We're sailing in international waters. You have no jurisdiction."

"I can wait until we dock in Europe."

Janus looked at her, shaking his head. "You really don't get it, do you?"

"What's to get?"

"Check the date."

"If you're referring to the fact that yesterday was Friday the thirteenth, I don't believe in that superstitious stuff."

"Well, you should."

Melika wasn't sure how to respond.

Janus said, "Because it's not about the cargo."

"What does *that* mean?"

He laughed.

"You're going down, Janus," she said.

"Really?" He banged the button for the elevator and the doors opened immediately. Inside, he hit another button. The green exterior light indicated he was heading up.

"That's not what I meant," Melika said.

"I know."

She could hear his strange cackle fading, the elevator ascending.

Melika stared at the doors. "What the fuck?"

* * * *

"Where you been?" Abram asked.

"I had to go pee." Melika pulled her chair up to the captain's table.

The waiter had cleared the table except for a pitcher of cream, a dish of sugar, and two fresh coffees.

Abram glanced over his shoulder. "The washroom's that way," he said pointing to the back of the restaurant. "Not that way." He looked toward the door leading to the elevators.

"I found one. Who cares?" She took a sip of coffee. "Oh, God, decaf." She pushed her cup aside. "Where's the waiter? I need real coffee."

"How about we get out of here?" Abram said. "Maybe get a little fresh air."

"Sure." She immediately got to her feet. "Let's find John and Judy. The *Titanic* fanatics." She made air quotes with her fingers. "Maybe they'd share their joint."

Abram laughed, standing as well. "You noticed, too, huh?"

"Yeah. I wonder where they got it."

"We should find out. You could use it. I mean, you're wound pretty tight." He tucked his chair under the table. "Especially for someone who's just come from the washroom."

"Well, you know, I had a lot to work out."

"Okay, too much information," he said. "Let's go."

"Whoa, hold up."

"What?"

A teenager wearing a white sailor's uniform was heading toward them, wanting to run but trying to keep a disciplined, albeit hurried, walk.

"Michael, take it easy," Melika said when he got to the table.

"Sorry, Miss Jones. I had to tell you."

"Michael, we discussed this. I'm not Miss Jones. I'm Melika."

"Yes, ma'am."

Abram was surprised she didn't correct the kid for using that name as well.

"What's up?" Melika said.

"There's been a fire." He sounded more excited than afraid, busting to share the news.

"Shhh, just take it easy. Have a seat."

He quickly sat and started to explain before Melika and Abram had pulled their chairs back up to the table.

"In the coal bunker," Michael said.

"Coal bunker?" Melika asked.

"It's not a real coal bunker," Michael explained. "It's the museum, the *Titanic* exhibit."

"How bad?"

"Bad. Gutted. The captain's down there now."

"Jesus," Abram said. "Shouldn't we have heard a fire alarm?"

Michael turned to Abram. The kid had been so focused on telling his story to Melika that he seemed surprised to find someone else at the table. "No, sir, mister …?"

"Abram."

"No, sir, Mr. Abram. The room automatically sealed. The sprinklers kept it under control until the firemen put it out. There was no danger to the passengers."

"Still," Abram said, "you think they would've stopped the ship as a precaution."

Michael shrugged. He looked anxiously at Melika.

So did Abram.

She was shaking her head. "It seems nothing will stop this ship."

"That's for sure," Michael said. "I just saw Mr. Janus. He's all in a panic."

"Janus?" she asked.

"Yeah." Michael didn't continue but looked uncertainly at Abram.

"It's okay," Melika said. "You can talk in front of Abram."

"Just now," Michael pointed his thumb over his shoulder toward the elevator, "Mr. Janus was on his way to the bridge while I was coming down to find you. He was yelling at one of the officers to get an S-Stealth out here. Right away."

"A Sikorsky Stealth," she said.

"That's a helicopter, right?" Michael asked.

"Yeah. Expensive, but quiet."

"You think someone wants off the ship?" Michael asked.

Melika didn't answer.

"Like Mr. Janus?" Michael said.

"No, I don't think he's going anywhere."

"He was pretty mad, though. After he yelled at the officers, he went to see Captain Bartlett. I could see them talking. The captain got pretty steamed, too." Michael looked at his watch. "I gotta go. Curfew. I'm supposed to be in my cabin every night by 21:00 hours." He gave Melika an under-the-hat, half-hidden salute, then turned to Abram and nodded. "Nice to meet you, Mr. Abram," he said.

"Likewise."

Michael hustled out of the restaurant.

"Who was that kid?" Abram asked.

"He's the cabin boy. Works for the crew, running errands." Melika dropped back in her chair, scratching her head.

"Looks like he's working for you, too."

She nodded, obviously preoccupied with Michael's information.

"You think Janus is up to something?" Abram asked.

"With the helicopter, you mean?"

"Yeah," Abram said.

"I think he's got a package he's desperate to get rid of."

"Something to do with the fire?"

"I don't think so. But who knows anymore?" She hit the table. "Damn. I'm losing it. I forgot to ask Michael how the fire started."

"Maybe a cigarette."

"Cigarette?" She sat up. "Why would you say that?"

"Hey, don't jump all over me." Abram raised his hands, surrendering. "After arson, smoking is the number one cause of fire."

"Arson?" She narrowed her eyes.

So did Abram. "This comes as a surprise to you?"

She shook her head, settling back. "No, of course not."

"You want to hear something funny?"

"What?" she asked, her voice lacking its usual muscle.

"It's ironic, that's all. In *Titanic*'s day, a fire smoldering in a ship's coal bunker was commonplace. Some say *Titanic* sailed with one."

"So?"

"Now the *Sister*'s had a fire in her bunker as well."

She gave him an impatient look. "It was a display, Abram. Part of Janus's museum."

"Yeah, but what was in the coal bunker museum?"

Melika shrugged. "Coal, I guess."

"That may not be as funny as it sounds. Salvagers recovered a lot of *Titanic*'s coal from the ocean floor. I bet some of it was on display or for sale."

"I don't know. The museum was gutted."

"Think about it. *Titanic*'s coal burning in *Titan's Sister*, a hundred years later?"

"So?" Melika asked again.

"That's just plain creepy."

"Is there anything about this ship that isn't?"

Abram wanted to defend the *Sister*, but the parallels were troubling him too. "First the guy in the funnel," he said. "Then the radio. Now the fire." He hadn't forgotten about the men giving him messages. In his jacket pocket, he carried the numbers he'd written down.

"What's going through that head of yours, Abram?"

He was wondering whether he should show her the messages. If he did, she'd press him for background information that Abram didn't want to share. On the other hand, she might know what the sequence of numbers meant.

Reaching into his coat pocket, he pulled out the piece of White Star stationery.

Melika grabbed it before he had a chance to change his mind.

"Those numbers mean anything to you?" he asked.

She studied them. "Where'd they come from?"

"There are two messages," he said, pointing to each line.

"I can see that. Who gave them to you?"

"I can't say for sure. Actors, maybe?" He shrugged. "Another throwback to *Titanic*'s era?"

"More of Janus's games." She gave Abram back his note. "Let me know if you get any others," she said and stood up. "I gotta run. Morgan will want to know about the helicopter." Hesitating, she tucked her chair under the table with the help of her foot. "Do you remember what they looked like? The actors, I mean?"

"One was a skinny white guy, the other guy was bigger. Like the captain, sort of, but older."

She thought for a second. "I got this book," she said. "*Titanic for Dummies.*"

"No way? There's one of those books for everything."

She shrugged. "Lot of dummies in the world, I guess. Anyway, it's got some pictures I want you to look at."

"A picture book?" Abram tried to lighten her mood. "And you haven't finished coloring it yet?"

Melika was dead serious. "I'll bring it over tonight. I want to see if your two messengers look like anyone from back then. If I spot them on board, I'd like to have a little chat with them."

He looked at her, intrigued, a slight smile on his face, repeating her words over in his head, making sure he'd heard her right. *I'll bring it over tonight.* This wasn't about the book. And Abram didn't need Melika to protect him. She knew that. She wanted to come to his cabin. But not without her safety net, a cop-like excuse to fall back on.

He caught her eyes before she looked away. "You're sure about this?" he asked.

"Give me an hour."

Chapter Fifteen

Ignoring punctuation and capital letters, Melika banged out an e-mail to Morgan, paraphrasing the conversation she'd had with Janus after dinner. In so many words, Janus had admitted bribing the fire marshal to close the dock fire investigation. Janus had also confessed to hiding funnel man's body. But the worst was Janus's admission that he'd found Blake Tellemann before the launch. Thinking Tellemann was already dead, Janus decided it would be okay to report the incident after the *Sister* was afloat. All to keep his ship on schedule. Why was that so damned important? She couldn't get him to admit to the sand. In fact, he'd intimated his rush had nothing to do with the cargo. Probably it was just Janus being his usual flaky self. Morgan was likely right—Janus wanted to get his cargo overseas and reap his profits before word leaked out.

In a postscript, she asked Morgan to check the flight plans registered out of Norfolk. She wanted to confirm her suspicions that Janus was airlifting funnel man back to port. He seemed to be taking her threat that she could turn the ship around because of the man on ice seriously.

Fingers poised to start a second postscript, she took a breath and hit send instead. She was going to mention the fire on board, as well as the *Sister*'s radio problems. But coupling these two things with the man in the funnel made the parallels to *Titanic* seem more than just coincidence. Also, there were Abram's messages. Four numbers, two digits each. Until she could tie some logical explanation to these incidents, she wasn't going to tell Morgan. She didn't want Morgan to think she was losing it.

Needing to rest her eyes and clear her head, she logged off her computer, stripped off her clothes, and slipped into the terry bathrobe she'd left on her unmade bed. If the ship didn't sell these robes, she'd pack hers by accident when they hit land. It was the most comfortable garment she'd worn in a long time.

She had just closed her eyes when the phone rang.

"I got your message," Morgan said.

"Morgan, for Pete's sake. I sent you an e-mail so I wouldn't have to talk to you."

"I know."

"Then why are you bugging me?"

"Nothing was in your e-mail about what you found in the cargo holds. Remember? The cabin boy was taking you down to see the sand this afternoon?"

She blinked tiredness from her eyes. "Yeah, you're right." Reaching to the nightstand, she picked up a sandwich bag with a handful of Janus's precious cargo inside. "I found a little on the floor. It's heavy," she said. "Pretty, though."

"Why? What's it look like?"

"It's the color you'd get mixing ground-up charcoal with baking powder."

"Baking powder? You mean you found cocaine?"

"No," Melika said. "Not in the sample I've got anyway. But it's the perfect cover."

"How so?"

"According to Michael, the sand was loaded onto the ship in bags, like sand bags. Janus could've laced a few of those bags with the coke mixture. At customs, the dogs wouldn't be able to sniff it out because of the charcoal. And, if by chance one of the illicit bags were picked during a visual inspection, the coke would be indistinguishable."

"Yeah. But why risk it?" Morgan asked. "If customs found so much as a gram, they'd confiscate his entire cargo."

"Man, I'd love to see that. But you're right. It's a long shot."

"Well, based on our suspicions that he traffics out of South America with his ships, I might be able to get English customs to take a solid look at what he's carrying on the *Sister*. If they find anything, I'll have Janus on his way home for indictment on the first ship out. How's that sound?"

"Serve him right if it was his own boat," Melika said.

"Still not taking to life on the high seas, huh?"

"I'm not sure what to think."

"If it'll make you feel any better," Morgan said, "I checked with NOAA. There are no icebergs in your path."

"Great."

"You can thank global warming. Chunks of ice from Greenland don't drift that far south anymore."

"I'll be sure to send a letter to my head-in-the-proverbial-sand congressman."

"Mellow out, Jones. I can take it from here. Good work, by the way, getting Janus to admit his involvement in the Tellemann incident."

"Thanks."

"So reward yourself. Have some fun for a change. Incidentally, how's it going with Abram?"

"I guess I'm done with him."

"Are you sure?"

"Morgan, stop it. You're supposed to be my partner. Not my matchmaker."

"Will you relax? Man, stuff a lump of coal up your butt and you'd shit diamonds."

"Coal? Why did you say coal?"

"You tell me. You're the one who taught me the expression."

"I gotta go, Morgan."

"See ya soon, kiddo."

She hung up.

She looked around her cabin.

What a mess.

To protect the confidentiality of the investigation, she hadn't let the cleaning staff into the room. Her bed wasn't made. Towels hung over chairs. And scattered on the dresser and night tables were water glasses, coffee mugs, and the telltale rings they left behind. That wasn't the worst of it. Files littered her bed, their contents strewn about or falling on the floor. If her end of the investigation was pretty much wrapped up, as Morgan suggested, her files, all her precious pieces of evidence, her theories, and her conclusions would be filed and indexed, neatly tucked away and tidy.

Maybe Morgan was right. Maybe she was burning out.

Maybe she should've gotten help a long time ago. To clear away the clutter. To make sense of the chaos that had become her life. She envied Abram. His innate confidence. His stability. His capacity to live life without fear of spiraling out of control. Not long ago, she would've said the same thing about herself. But who was she kidding? She didn't know any other way to deal with life except to try to outrun it.

Chiding herself, she tapped the headboard with the back of her head. *Why did I tell Abram about the plane crash, anyway? I vowed never to talk about it with anyone.* Not even Morgan, although I'm sure he knows. *How could I take it back, tell Abram to erase it from his memory? How could I erase it from my own memory?*

She blinked several times, feeling something foreign in her eyes. *Tears? Damn it.* She sniffed. *Why now? Why after all these years?*

Because something has tripped me up, left me confused, unable to put together a picture from the pieces around me. I've fallen. And how will I pick myself back up? The way I always do. Find the perp. Assign blame where it belongs.

And where are the answers?

Somewhere on this goddamn son-of-a-bitch ship.

Chapter Sixteen

In some ways, Abram wished he hadn't fallen asleep after the large meal at the captain's table. The taste of coffee had grown stale in his mouth, his muscles weren't keen to respond to the commands of his groggy brain, and, as he sat up, a prolonged burp, tasting of aged cheese, nuts, and wine, rose from his stomach. But as he swung his legs over the side of his bed and glanced at the clock, he realized the time had passed quickly. It was almost eleven. Melika had said she'd be by around that time.

With only the faint illumination from the floor lights, Abram shuffled to the bathroom, turned on the hot water, and bent toward the mirror. In the dim light, he caught a glimpse of an older-looking man with spirals of grey hair in his sideburns and skin puckering near his eyes. A reflection of his father. That wasn't so bad. Clay had spirit, conviction, strength—qualities Pop would never lose even if his final years left him crippled and confused. Abram hoped he could maintain a fraction of Pop's resilience.

Leaning back from the sink, Abram blinked several times, trying to moisten his bloodshot eyes. He noticed movement in the mirror, outside the bathroom door. He turned. Nothing was behind him.

A trick of the strained light?

Maybe it was Pop. Or Melika.

He closed his eyes, then opened them and looked from corner to corner in the reflecting glass.

There it was again, outside the bathroom door.

Instinctively, Abram scanned the bathroom for something to protect himself. A safety razor wouldn't do much. Would his fists do him any good?

With short, quick steps, he rounded the corner from the bathroom, flicked on the lamp by the bed, and braced himself. Hiding in the uneven illumination was not some elusive thug ready to jump him. Rather, a dark, middle-aged man stood near the cabin door. He was tall and confident-looking, with his shirtsleeves rolled up.

Abram lowered his arms and exhaled. "I figured you'd show up eventually."

No response.

"How'd you get into my room? Jesus, what's with the three of you?"

The man turned slightly, his eyes shifting toward the bathroom.

"No, not this time," Abram said. He took a step forward. "I'm not taking my eyes off you until I get some answers."

The man reached for the knob on the cabin door.

"Wait. Just tell me what you want."

Instead, the man looked toward the bathroom again.

Out of the corner of his eye, Abram saw grayish fingers of fog curling along the floor toward him.

For a moment, Abram wasn't sure of the source. He wanted to move away, to escape whatever was reaching for him, but he stayed where he was, fearing how the man would react.

"Why don't you just talk to me?" Abram asked. "Tell me what this is all about."

Nothing.

Moisture dotted Abram's cheek. It was warm and smelled pure and clean. Mist. That's all it was, he convinced himself. He hadn't turned off the hot water faucet.

Steam drifted from the bathroom, climbing the walls on currents of cooler air. Abram clenched his fists in frustration. "Talk to me, damn it!" he said.

The man hurried out the door. Abram ran after him, careful not to trip on the duvet piled on the floor. He reached the door and yanked it open only to find an empty hallway outside.

"Fuck! Jesus Effing Christ!"

Kicking the blanket, then the bed, wanting to punch the wall but restraining himself, he headed back to the bathroom.

"Shit." Not only was the hot water running, it had filled the sink and overflowed onto the floor. Abram tossed several towels on the marble tile before turning off the faucet.

The towel he was standing on slipped. He tried to correct his balance, but something written on the mirror startled him. In the millisecond it took to register what it was, his foot went sideways. He grabbed for the sink and missed.

He fell, his head cracking on the white marble floor.

His eyes fluttered once, twice, filling with darkness. For a moment, he struggled against the murkiness that was encompassing him. There was no way out. He had to let go.

His muscles went slack.

Then there was nothing.

* * * *

A cold bottle of Dasani in hand, her face still wet from an icy splash of water, Melika stretched out on the bed, her case files surrounding her.

"Goddamn son-of-a-bitch ship," she repeated.

It's where her troubles had started. Where she'd met Abram. And where her investigation had somehow devolved into a jumble in her head. Morgan might believe their case was under control. But he wasn't on the *Sister*. Janus was right. This ship had ghosts. Vague, shape-shifting feelings nagged at her, surrounded her, trying to convince her that something ominous hid in the heart of the vessel. Something criminal with a newborn face.

Who? Or what?

Surprise me, she thought. With no logical place to start, she covered her eyes and picked up a file at random. She'd go through all the files if she had to. Sometimes it happened that way in investigative work. You couldn't make sense of things. Then you'd stumble across the missing link, something overlooked, a small piece of evidence that completed the overall picture.

"The answer is ..." she said, holding up the folder. "Oh, great." It was the backgrounds of the officers on board. She'd been through this file at least twice before. Everybody had checked out.

Captain Timothy J. Bartlett had been a seaman for twenty-two years. He'd had a relatively uneventful career except for a freak accident aboard an oil tanker where he busted up his knee trying to save a fellow seaman. Melika had noticed his slight limp at dinner.

Despite Bartlett's disability, he'd attained the rank of captain ten years ago, at an early age according to the file, and he had been assigned to a variety of vessels. *Titan's Sister* was a logical career move for him.

Chief Officer Hank Tannara had worked for Bartlett a number of years. Bartlett had always requested, and had always been granted, his pick of chief officer, and he inevitably picked Tannara.

Nor was there anything unusual about the assignments of the remaining officers. First Officer Bill McNeil, Third Officer Herb Jacobs, and Fourth Officer Joe Geller were all assigned to *Titan's Sister* by the union's rules of seniority. Second Officer Chuck Blair and Fifth Officer Harry Graves were hired by lottery. The remaining officer, Sixth Officer Jimmy Pearce, was a last-minute assignment after he was let go by a failing merchant line.

Melika leafed through the folder, nothing new standing out.

Covering her eyes once again, she reached for another file. This time she picked up her notes on Abram.

"Okay, Mr. Harwood. Why has fate drawn you from my little travel bag of tricks?"

He had a record that she'd never asked him about.

"What else?" she said, closing her eyes and thinking. She couldn't put it together. She grabbed a pen and a piece of stationery to list the major events in the history of the *Sister*. Alongside each, she'd note Abram's involvement. If any.

"Day One." She underlined it. Abram was an integral part of building the ship from day one.

"The Launch." Abram's best friend died in a freak accident.

"The Dock Fire." It had started in Abram's tent after one of his propane tanks was left open. The only injury was Abram.

"Funnel man."

Wait a minute.

Melika went back to the fire. What about the skinny white guy wearing an old-fashioned suit? Abram was sure they'd been rushed to a waiting ambulance together. Regardless, neither the rescue team nor the paramedics remembered the man. She and Morgan figured the toxic smoke had messed with Abram's memory.

Or maybe the mystery man was one of the actors Abram had talked about when he showed her the two cryptic messages this evening. She hadn't told Abram, but it was obvious to her what the sequence of numbers meant.

She picked up Tellemann's book and scanned through it, stopping at a page that listed the location of *Titanic*'s wreck. It confirmed her theory. The four numbers in Abram's messages were map coordinates. Granted, the one she'd stumbled upon didn't match either of Abram's. But they were damn close.

She snapped the book shut and stretched. Why would an actor risk his life in a fire to deliver a map coordinate? She tapped the book. He wouldn't. Maybe Abram was playing games, making up the men and their messages. Maybe he knew a hell of a lot more about *Titanic* and the *Sister* than he was letting on. After all, it was Abram who said that *Titanic* had a coal fire. He'd reminded her of the other similarities as well. Funnel man. The dead radio. She wished she could go back and read all his reactions to these various things. She should've been more vigilant. That's what *had* made her so good at what she did. She looked at everyone as a potential suspect. She'd seen people out of context and been able to separate them from their immediate environments. She could picture them in places where other people, innocent people, didn't fit. Abram was different. He couldn't be pigeonholed.

What had blinded her to the obvious?

Janus. He had always been the focus of her investigation. He was at the heart of it. Now, so was Abram. Was the relationship between Abram and Janus more than just a working one? At the captain's table, she'd noticed they were on a first-name basis. Sort of. No one called Bruce Janus anything except Janus.

Standing, Melika made loose fists and punched them lightly together.

Hadn't Abram Harwood, just last night, leaned across the table with a hot, teasing, cognac-laden breath and told her she should be watching *him*?

Not Janus, he'd said. No. *It's me. I'm the one you need to watch.* He never did tell her why.

What else? Think. She rubbed her forehead.

The boxes in the hold. They were welded. Abram was a welder. She was reaching. Or was she? Think forest, not trees.

"Yes!" she said. "I got it!"

Grabbing the phone, she quickly dialed Abram's number.

One ring.

How should she handle this?

Two rings.

Interrogate him as a suspect?

Three rings.

But maybe he was innocent.

Four rings.

"Shit," she dropped the phone into the cradle and immediately picked it up again, dialing Clay.

"Come on, Clay," she said.

He answered on the third ring.

"Have you seen Abram?" she asked.

"Melika?" Clay cleared his throat. "No, Abram's not here. You all right?"

"Where is he?"

"I don't know. Just a second. I'll see if the adjoining door is open."

Melika tossed off her terry robe and grabbed the only garments within reach. Cradling the phone with her shoulder, she slipped into the dress she'd worn for dinner and pulled her nylon windbreaker over top. Her runners were handy as well. Still waiting, she snatched up her gun, lock pick, and ... she hesitated. Yes, she'd better take Tellemann's book, too.

She was about to hang up when Clay came back on the line.

"Quick, come quick!" he said.

Chapter Seventeen

When Abram opened his eyes, he saw a figure standing over him and sensed movement off to the side. His first instinct was to scramble backward, but he could barely move.

He heard a voice. It was familiar.

"Just take it easy. You're going to be fine."

Melika?

The room came into focus. He was on the floor of the bathroom; Melika was beside him, and his father sat on the edge of the tub, rubbing his knees anxiously. Abram could feel a cool cloth on his forehead and a towel rolled up under his neck.

He struggled to find his voice. "What happened?"

"You tell us," Melika said.

He tried to look around. A throbbing pain shot from his head down his neck. "Damn it."

Taking hold of his arm and shoulder, Melika said, "Let's see if we can get you up."

With her help, Abram pulled himself into a sitting position. The bright light in the room bleached out the objects, telling him he'd sat up too fast.

As the normal flow of blood returned to his head, he realized something else. "My arm. I can't feel my arm!"

Melika held his weight. "Just take it easy. It's probably asleep. Lord knows how long you've been lying on it."

Abram grimaced as an army of pins and needles struck him. He made a fist, reassuring himself he could move his fingers. But the pain was like fire. The furrowing of his brow caused a new sensation, and he immediately forced his hand to his head.

"You got a nasty bump," Clay said. "Knocked you out."

"I don't ... I don't remember." Abram looked at Melika.

"Did someone do this to you?" she asked. "Was someone in your cabin?"

"I'm not sure."

"Think, Abram."

He rubbed his eyes. "I don't know. Maybe."

Melika took a deep breath. "Okay, let's get you up and into the other room. Then we'll talk."

With Clay on one side and Melika on the other, Abram staggered to his feet. He felt dizzy as he took his first few guarded steps.

When they were nearly out of the bathroom, Abram hesitated. He looked over his shoulder and into the mirror. He remembered something.

"What is it, son?"

"Nothing," Abram said, once again concentrating on walking.

They helped him to the side of the bed, where he sat and held the damp cloth to his head.

Melika poured Abram a glass of water while Clay headed to the cabin door. "Where the hell is that damn steward with that damn ice?" he said, looking up and down the hallway.

Abram didn't want water. He tried to concentrate and recover more of his short-term memory. "There was steam."

Melika set the glass on the nightstand. "Steam?"

"On the mirror. I could see ... numbers."

"Let me guess. Four numbers. Two digits each."

Abram nodded, though it pained his head. "The last message. It's gotta be."

Clay yelled over his shoulder, "I'm going to get the damn ice myself." The door swung shut behind him.

"All right, Abram," Melika said, pulling a chair close to the bed and sitting. "Let's start with this supposed last message." Her tone was official, detective-like.

He pointed to the end of the bed. "Is that the book?" he asked.

"Yeah." She passed it to him.

Abram ran his fingertips over the cover. He recognized it. Blake's book. The one Melika had stolen from his condo. "*This is your book for dummies?*" he asked.

"Turn to page 167. You'll see why."

Abram still felt light-headed and had a hard time keeping his eyes focused. He didn't have any trouble making out what Melika pointed to, however. "Of course," he said. "It's obvious. Map coordinates."

"Yeah. But what for?"

Abram tossed Melika the book and put the cool cloth back to his head. "You're the detective. You find out."

She caught Blake's book before it hit the floor. "What makes you think your numbers are in here?"

"You got any better ideas? Think of it as a clue. Maybe they're locations of other ships or something."

"I don't get it," Melika said. "What would ships in 1912 have to do with you?"

He shrugged and grimaced at the same time. "Where's Pop with that ice?"

Melika put one hand on her hip. "If you know something, spill it."

"Just see what you can find in the book," Abram said.

She paced while she skimmed the pages then stopped in midstep. "Those numbers are warnings. They're not obscure messages from the past warning you about the future. They're locations where ships on *Titanic*'s route spotted ice."

"Ice warnings?" Abram held out his hand. "You mean *Titanic* knew about the danger ahead of her?"

"See for yourself." Melika gave him the book.

Running his finger under each line to keep his eyes from drifting, he read each message. "Look at the controversy surrounding the three warnings." He gave her back the book. His head was swimming. "Check out the first one. The one I got from the guy at the shipyard fire."

"Right, the man only you saw."

"Yeah," Abram said, letting Melika's implication pass. He nodded at the book, pressing Melika to read the circumstances of the first message.

She took a minute. "Interesting," she said. "It's a message from a German steamer, *Amerika*, reporting the proximity of large icebergs. Apparently, it was never charted on the bridge."

"Look at the second one."

Melika hesitated. After a second, she lowered her head to read about the next warning. "A ship called the *Mesaba* indicated large icebergs in *Titanic*'s immediate vicinity." She held the book a little closer. "*Titanic*'s radio operator didn't understand how important the message was and put it aside until things got less busy."

Abram nodded. "The radio operators weren't crewmen. They were hired to send and receive passengers' messages."

Melika read about Abram's third ice warning without prompting. "According to this, your third message was *Titanic*'s last warning. A cargo ship, the *Californian*, had stopped because of all the ice. When the ship tried to warn *Titanic*, *Titanic*'s radio operators told her to keep out because they were working so hard to clear a backlog of passengers' messages."

"No doubt the backlog was a result of the broken radio from earlier in the day."

"Yeah. That's why they were so busy," Melika said.

"It all fits."

Melika closed the book. "Thirty minutes later, *Titanic* hit the iceberg."

Abram tapped his chin with his fist. "Thirty minutes," he said. "What time is it now?"

"A little after eleven. Why?"

"Give me the book."

Abram fanned through the book, stopping briefly to take a quick look at any page with a picture. "Seeing if I can recognize any of the three men may not be such a stupid idea."

"Stupid idea?"

"The excuse you gave me after dinner at the captain's table to drop by my cabin later on."

"Excuse me?"

"Think about it," he said. "If someone was trying to warn you about the fate of a ship, who would it be?"

"An excuse to come to your cabin? What's that supposed to mean?"

"It'd be the key players. The ship's owner, Bruce Ismay. The shipbuilder's representative on board, Thomas Andrews. And, of course, the captain. Edward J. Smith, the man ultimately responsible. The owner, shipbuilder, and captain. They'd know better than anybody the danger we face."

Melika's arms were crossed tightly against her chest, her back straight, her chin down, and eyes narrowed. "First of all," she said, "I don't need an excuse to come to your cabin. Second, the fate of *Titanic* has nothing to do with this ship, if that's what you think these warnings are about. And third, even if it did, there are no such things as ghosts. The key players are not haunting this ship."

Abram kept flipping pages.

"Abram, think about it," she said. "Ghosts, for Christ's sake?"

Clay came puffing through the cabin door, muttering about the scarcity of ice machines and the incompetence of stewards. He handed Abram an ice pack.

"Thanks, Pop," Abram said without looking up from the book.

"What'd I miss?" Clay asked.

"Your son believes in ghosts," Melika said.

Clay shrugged. "Could be worse." He turned to Abram. "How's the head?"

"Sore."

"I'll get you some of my painkillers." Clay was off again, this time through the adjoining door to his cabin.

Abram closed the book. "It'd be a stretch to say my guys look like the three from *Titanic*."

"Good, no ghosts."

Abram wasn't quick to agree.

"Look," Melika said, "someone is trying to scare you."

"It's working."

"Maybe you saw something you weren't supposed to when the ship was being built. Think back. Even as recent as the night before the *Sister* set sail. Are you a threat to anyone? Like Janus?"

"Janus? What's he got to do with anything?"

"Could he be the one who got into your room tonight?"

"No way. This guy was bigger, tougher, about my height." Abram thought a moment. "If any of the three men looked like Janus, it was the first guy, the guy at the shipyard fire."

Melika shook her head. "Janus was safe and sound in one of the firefighting command vehicles, nearly hysterical because his ship was on fire."

"I know." Abram rubbed his temples. "What time is it?"

"Five minutes after the last time you asked."

"Find out what happened after *Titanic* got the last message, will you?"

She picked up the book. "When are you going to learn how to read?"

"When Pop finds his painkillers."

Melika read to herself. She shook her head. "Everything was against them."

"What do you mean?"

"Twenty-four/seven monitoring of the radio wasn't required back then. When *Titanic* told the *Californian* to keep out, her radio operator went to bed. The *Californian* never heard the SOS, even though she was so close."

"Anybody else in the area?"

"The *Mesaba* and a Cunard liner, *Carpathia*. Both heard the SOS, or CQD as it was called at the time, and headed for *Titanic*'s reported position."

Pill bottle in hand, Clay was back.

Abram popped two painkillers without water.

"Listen to this," Melika said. "It'll make the hair on the back of your neck stand on end."

She read the passage aloud.

> *Titanic*'s distress messages were becoming more frantic. Despite the darkness of the night, no moon to watch over them, no lights on the horizon, except one, a possible masthead light flickering to the north, the night was alive with telegraph messages. Come at once, Titanic sang out. Putting women off in small boats, engine room full up to the boilers.
>
> In response came the voice of the *Baltic*, over two hundred miles away, saying we are rushing to you. Others joined in the frantic rescue: the *Mount Temple*, we are reversing our ship; the *Olympic*, *Titanic*'s sister, some five hundred miles away, am lighting up all possible boilers as fast as we can.
>
> Well into the night the drama continued. At 2:17 AM, the *Virginian* reports hearing *Titanic* call CQ, then nothing, her signal ending as though the power were suddenly switched off. *Titanic* has foundered. And yet the world has not yet realized. The *Carpathia* radios, if you are there we are firing rockets. The *Birma* sends a message saying, steaming full speed to you. Shall arrive at six in the morning. Hope you are safe ... we are only fifty miles now. But *Titanic* is gone. And except for twenty helpless lifeboats, the debris from her decks, and a thousand or so people wrapped futilely in cork life jackets against a frigid sea, there was nothing now to mark her true position.

Abram rubbed his neck. "What do they mean, true position?"

Melika flipped to the next page. "This is interesting. In 1992, after *Titanic*'s wreck was found, Southampton's Department of Transport commissioned an investigation regarding the *Californian*. It was always believed that she was close enough to save most of the passengers if only she'd heard *Titanic*'s SOS or responded to the flares that were fired."

"And?"

"Working back from the location of the wreck and allowing for the ocean's current, apparently *Titanic* was not where she thought she was. The 1992 investigation concluded that the *Californian* would not have reached *Titanic* in time, regardless of effort."

Abram removed the ice pack from his head and tossed it lightly in his hand. "One thing on top of another," he said.

"Come the bitter end, less than a third of the passengers survived."

Abram stared at the book. Blake's book. If the chain of events had been broken ... if one thing had been different. He stood. "I've got to get to the bridge."

"What for?"

"The captain needs to know about these warnings."

"He's not going to buy into your paranoia."

"I think he might." Abram wobbled a bit but managed a few steps from the bed.

Melika put her arm out, stopping him. "Why, what do you know?"

"I know these guys have been trying to warn me ever since the launch."

"And you think the captain has also been threatened? Not by the same guys, surely?"

Abram shrugged. He wasn't certain. Maybe. Why not? Who cares? "I owe it to Blake."

"Abram, this is crazy." Melika grabbed his arm. "We need to get you to sick bay."

Abram was quick to pull away. "I don't need my head examined, if that's what you're getting at."

Melika didn't back down. "I'm not going to the captain with this nonsense."

"Fine. Stay here."

Clay took a stance next to Abram, facing Melika.

Melika didn't look away from Abram. "First, answer me this. Did you work on some last-minute fabrication of crates for the hold?"

"So what?"

"Do you know what they were for?"

"The crates? No."

"Let me help you out," she said, defaulting into interrogation mode. "Janus is shipping something he doesn't want anybody to know about. It's worth a hell of a lot of money. And I think you're involved."

Abram tried to push past, heading for the door. "I don't know anything about the cargo," he told her. "Nor do I care."

"I think you might."

Clay immediately interrupted. "What the hell's that supposed to mean?"

Melika answered Clay, though she kept her eyes on Abram. "Abram found out about the cargo. He's blackmailing Janus."

Clay nearly choked on his words. "You've got to be kidding!"

"Ask your son."

Abram held Melika's stare.

Clay kept at her. "What's so damn important about this cargo?"

"Does your son know anything about precious metals, like platinum?"

"Platinum?" Clay asked.

"What about drugs?" Melika said. "Coke?"

Abram had heard enough. "This is ridiculous." He pushed closer to the door.

"Is it?" Melika asked, holding her ground. "Maybe your three buddies have a better explanation."

"Maybe *I've* got a better explanation," Clay said. "Maybe when he was working on the crates, he overheard something. Maybe somebody is trying to scare him to keep him quiet."

"Or perhaps your son is making it all up. Maybe he's crazier than Janus."

"That's enough!" Abram said. He finally had the strength to get around Melika and made sure she knew it.

She grabbed his shoulder.

Abram wrenched free.

She tried catching his arm.

He faced her, seized her wrist, and pushed her back, holding her at a distance.

Now *she* tried to wrench free.

Abram tightened his grip, knowing he was cutting off the flow of blood to her hand.

"Abram, for Christ's sake …" Melika said.

He held his grip, hoping she'd feel his frustration and know what it was like to be on the other side, to be handcuffed by someone, at the mercy of their temperament.

She eased up, no longer fighting him, her arm loose. "Just take it easy, okay?" she said. "We can talk this out."

"I don't think so."

"Abram, relax, okay."

Maybe she sees that she's being unreasonable, that her frustration has more to do with her inner turmoil than with the ship. He let her go.

For a moment, she said nothing, rubbing her wrist. "Shit, Harwood," she said, toughening up. "What was that about?"

He shook his head. It was over. "You really don't get it do you?" Abram said.

"Janus asked exactly the same question," she said.

"Smart man," Abram said. He turned and had taken a step away from Melika when a heavy knock—three successive thumps—came from the other side of the door.

"Shit, what now?" Abram checked the peephole and didn't hesitate to open up. It was an officer. Second Officer Blair, according to his name tag.

He addressed Melika directly. "The captain wants you on the bridge, ma'am."

"What for?"

He turned to Abram. "You, too, Mr. Harwood."

Abram pushed into the hallway. "Never mind, what for," he said. "Let's go."

Chapter Eighteen

Although the subdued light and low hum of instruments should have provided a tranquil background, the tension was obvious when Abram reached the bridge with Melika, Second Officer Blair, and Clay close behind.

First Officer McNeil stood stiffly at the window. The Sixth Officer, Pearce, sat quietly beside him.

Near Pearce, Bruce Janus was leaning against the console, his back to the window and his head down. He looked up briefly, his expression serious. But when his eyes locked on Melika's, Abram noticed something strange, a slight smile crossing Janus's face—a teasing look, almost.

The exchange didn't go unnoticed by Captain Bartlett. He was near the front of the bridge, looking over his shoulder. The soft, green glow of the displays cast an eerie light on his face, shrouding his eyes and shading the taut muscles in his neck and jaw. Without a word, he turned back to the window, his shoulders squared, his feet slightly apart, as though he were anticipating an angry and turbulent sea.

Outside, however, the night was quiet. Indiscernible from the black and breathless sky, the ocean held the *Sister* in a cold embrace.

It was Fourth Officer Geller, hustling through the rear door with a piece of paper in his hand, who broke the uneasy silence. "I've got it, Captain," he said.

"Finally. Let's hear it."

The Fourth Officer glanced in the direction of the civilians and hesitated.

"Now, Officer Geller," Bartlett said.

"Yes, sir. There was enough light, sir, to pick up the horizon. And with the telescopic sextant I was able to sight Polaris, Arcturus, and Mars." He shook his head. "It's odd. I've never seen a night like it."

The captain took a quick look out the window at the glass-like ocean. "I'm more concerned about where we are."

"Yes, sir. Forty-one degrees, forty-six minutes north, and fifty degrees, fourteen minutes west, sir."

Bartlett grabbed the paper from his officer.

Abram looked at Melika, but she was watching Janus. Janus had raised his head slightly, pinching the bridge of his nose as if troubled. Even so, a devilish look remained in his eyes.

Rereading the coordinates, Bartlett rubbed his forehead. "Then we *are* off course," he said.

"Yes, sir. I'm afraid so, sir," Geller responded.

"You're sure of this?"

"Yes, sir. I've checked twice. The UTC radio is down, but with the chronometer and those three star sights, I'm pretty sure we're a little to the south and several hours ahead of schedule. That'll put us over *Titanic*'s wreck at approximately twenty-four hundred hours."

An anxious look passed between Officers Pearce and McNeil.

Bartlett took a sharp breath. "Damn it, Geller. How is that possible? Before the navigational computer went down, we were right on time. And you yourself verified that against our speed and course."

"Yes, sir, I know. But when we lost the computer we also lost our speed indicator."

"And you compensated using the tachometers. Explain to me how even our redundant systems have failed us."

"Well, sir ..." Again Geller hesitated. "Sir, I'm not sure. I guess the tachs are reading wrong."

"Find out why. *Now.*"

Geller hurried to the nearest computer terminal and started banging on the keyboard.

The captain turned immediately to his sixth officer. "Status, Mr. Pearce."

"She's maintaining speed, sir. Bearing steady."

Abram took a step forward. "Captain Bartlett?"

Melika grabbed Abram's arm, but Abram pulled away.

The captain glanced over his shoulder. "I'll get to you and Ms. Jones in a minute."

"There's something you need to know," Abram insisted.

Bartlett turned to study Abram. Other than a muscle twitching in his jaw, the captain maintained the controlled, authoritative demeanor of a well-trained officer. But Abram believed experience had taught the captain something more. A sixth sense, perhaps, the ability to read the elements of nature and sense the warm hand of God or the deadly grip of an unforgiving spirit. Bartlett turned from the dark window, facing Abram. "What is it, Mr. Harwood?"

"According to Officer Geller's fix," Abram said, "we're within minutes of being at *Titanic*'s SOS position."

"No. The wreck is a few hours off."

"Where *Titanic* went down and where she thought she was are two different locations. *Titanic* had the wrong coordinates when she called for help."

"What are you saying?"

"Look at the clock."

Bartlett didn't take his eyes off Abram. "Pearce," the captain barked. "What time is it?"

"Twenty-three, thirty-eight, sir."

"Almost 11:40," Abram said. "The exact time *Titanic* struck the iceberg."

The captain shook his head. "That's too much of a coincidence, Mr. Harwood."

"Oh, for Christ's sake." It was Melika. She had Janus by the arm, dragging him toward Bartlett. "Tell the captain, Janus. Tell him you're playing another one of your games."

Janus pulled away. "She's crazy. Get her away from me."

The captain shot Janus a look to keep him quiet then focused on Melika. "What do you know, Ms. Jones?"

"I know Janus. *He's* the crazy one. A fanatic. This is another one of his games. Probably bribed your officer to report the wrong coordinates."

"That's ridiculous."

"Is it? Look at him. He's reveling in this. The realism of his cruise."

The captain glanced at Janus but kept the pressure on Melika. "This is not a game, Detective Jones. The incidents plaguing my ship are adding up. That's why I ordered you up here. I need to know why you're aboard. What you're investigating."

"What's being off course got to do with me?"

The captain's stare was penetrating. "You need to understand. My complete navigational system is down, along with the radar. Geller's fix suggests even our back-up systems have failed."

Melika took a step back.

"Captain?" It was Officer McNeil. He was clutching a telephone handset to his ear.

"What is it, McNeil?"

"Sir, engine room reports boilers five and six just came on line."

"What?"

"We're increasing speed, sir."

"On whose instructions?"

"No one's, sir. That's the thing." McNeil held up his hand as he listened to the voice on the other end of the phone. "Say again," he said. "Shit!" McNeil cut the conversation short. "Sir, we've got problems."

"What now?"

"The engine room panel just died. The chief engineer says he's got no control. He says the ship's running herself!"

"That's it." The captain said. "We're shutting down until we can get this figured out. Stop all engines."

"Stop all engines," Officer Pearce echoed.

Bartlett turned briefly to Janus, speaking low and even. "I'll have your hide if you've got anything to do with this."

Janus didn't respond. He was focusing nervously on the readings from boilers five and six.

The captain raised his voice. "I said stop all engines."

Again, the command was echoed.

There was no indication that the ship was slowing. If anything, the tachometer needles were edging higher.

Bartlett grabbed the phone to the engine room. "Did you not receive my order?" he shouted. A second or two later, he said, "I see," and hung up. He turned to his second officer, speaking quickly and concisely. "Blair, have more men posted on lookout. I want an officer in the crow's nest, two men at the bow, and a man on both the port and starboard bridge wings."

"Yes, sir." Blair darted out the back of the bridge.

"McNeil. Don't take your eyes off that water," the captain said, pointing out the forward windows. "Notify me immediately if you see anything."

McNeil shook his head, trying to understand. "What are we looking for?"

"Damn it, anything in our way. We're full speed ahead with no radar. Do as you're ordered—*now*."

Melika looked at Abram. "What's going on?"

Abram closed his eyes. "It's too late."

"Pearce," the captain barked. "Watch all the instruments. Feel the ship. I want to know if she starts doing anything other than what she's doing right now."

"Aye, aye, sir."

Bartlett turned firmly to Melika. "Detective Jones, I'm losing patience. Someone or something has taken over my ship. We're increasing speed, and I can't stop her. They're going to shut down the fuel pumps and close the valves manually to starve the engines, but ..."

The engine room phone rang. The captain grabbed it before McNeil. "All right," Bartlett said, responding to a loud voice. "What about shutting off the power?" He wrinkled his brow, listening. Finally, he said, "Okay. Do what you can, but be careful." Bartlett banged the handset into the cradle and turned back to Melika. "The fuel valves aren't responding. And the steam dampers are jammed. They can't shut off power to the fuel pumps because it stops the cooling pumps. It seems the only way to stop the *Sister* is by disengaging the shafts from the turbines. Not an easy job when we're running at twenty knots. Now, again, Detective Jones, who would have done this, and what was their purpose?"

Before Melika had a chance to speak, Pearce interjected. "Sir!" he yelled. "Boilers five and six are indicating high pressure."

"What? Boilers five and six are supposed to be locked off."

"Sir!" yelled Pearce. "The clock is blinking. It just turned 23:40 and it started to blink."

Bartlett turned to the bridge panel.

Melika took advantage of the distraction and moved away from the captain. She stood beside Abram and Clay.

Bruce Janus looked unbelievingly at needles indicating high pressure on boilers five and six, his childish expression gone. The color had drained from his face as if the round, analog gauges were the vacant eyes of a ghost staring back. "This can't be happening," he said. He grabbed the captain's arm. "Don't stop the engines."

"What?"

"Don't you see? The steam's building. If you stop the engines, there'll be too much back pressure. She'll blow."

Bartlett pulled his arm from Janus's grip. "I know that, you idiot. The relief valves will vent the pressure."

"No," Abram shouted, hurrying to Janus's side. "Remember? We didn't commission five and six. Look at the pressure. If the valves were set properly, they should've vented long ago."

"Damn it," Bartlett said. "I've got to stop this ship."

Abram took a step back from the front windows. "It's happening," he said. "It's happening all over again."

Melika's eyes darted from Bartlett to Abram. "What's happening?" she demanded.

Titan's Sister quietly answered. Without the slightest indication, without a flash, a spark, or a noise, the navigation board came dutifully to life.

"What the hell?" McNeil said.

"Thank heaven for small miracles," the captain responded. "Anything on the radar, Geller?"

"Radar clear, sir," the young fifth officer answered as he darted for his seat in front of the navigation console.

"Speed?"

"Registering exactly twenty-two point five knots, sir."

"What position is it giving us?"

"Well it's remarkable, captain. Both SINS and GPS are giving indications less than a minute off my sextant position."

"This can't be happening."

"Look sir! Look!" It was Pearce.

"What is it?"

"The collision avoidance system has just been activated."

"Geller, I thought you said nothing was on the radar."

"There isn't, sir. Nothing."

"How can the ship be reacting to something it can't see?"

"It can't, that's the thing. The radar is her eyes. But Pearce is right. The automatic target tracker is definitely watching something."

"Where's Blair?" the captain barked.

"Here, sir," came a voice from the back.

"Notify the look-outs that we're on automatic collision avoidance. I want to know the minute they see anything."

"Yes, sir."

"McNeil, anything from the engine room?"

"No, sir."

"Get them on the horn, now!"

"Yes, sir. Engine room here, sir." He handed Captain Bartlett the phone.

"What the hell is going on down there?" A moment later, a frustrated look crossed Bartlett's face, and he tightly clenched his fist. "Very well," he snapped, "keep trying." He slammed down the handset.

"Oh, my God," Geller whispered.

"What is it Geller?"

"The ship is changing course, sir."

"Blair, anything from your lookouts?"

"No, sir. Nothing, sir. Clear as a bell out there, sir."

Bartlett grabbed his binoculars and quickly scanned the horizon. He couldn't see anything either.

"Deactivate automatic collision avoidance," he ordered.

"Deactivating, sir. Jesus."

"A problem, Geller?"

"I can't get it off. I can't stop her."

Bartlett dropped the binoculars to his side. "Sound its movements."

"Yes, sir. She seems to be veering to port, sir, according to the compass, although the indicator says hard-a-starboard, maybe because—"

"The stop all engines indicator is on," Pearce interrupted.

"Watch the pressure on five and six."

"It's in the red, sir, as far as it can go. Wait … the full speed astern indicator just lit up."

A second later, the engine room phone burst to life. McNeil grabbed it. "Yes, we have it," he spoke into the receiver, then reported to the captain. "Engine room confirms that the engines are full speed astern, sir, although they don't know why."

The captain nodded, still staring ahead, his trained eyes watching for whatever the *Sister* was seeing. Even though they could feel the subtle vibration of full speed astern through her decks, the vessel was hardly beginning to slow. And only reluctantly was she swinging to port.

As though the crew could see the invisible obstacle that lay ahead, a sudden calm swept the bridge.

Seconds ticked away.

Abram watched the ocean ahead. Its coldness was unchanging. If it hadn't been for the bright stars disappearing on the right, he wouldn't have thought they were turning at all.

Clay and Melika gazed through the window while the captain and his officers watched the green letters of the digital compass flickering new readings. West became southwest, and the giant gradually altered course, boilers five and six deep in the red.

Ahead of them lay clear water, not a ripple on the ocean, not a vessel, light, or scrap of ice to be seen. And yet, from the very depths of *Titan's Sister*, words of disaster were being spoken once again.

Later, a passenger in the smoking room would say he saw ripples in his drink. A teacher five decks below wouldn't feel or hear anything unusual except for the sudden heave of the engines and a momentary increase in the vibration of his bed. But in the bowels of the ship, thunder would rock the starboard side, bursting in the ears of the engineers running frantically from the deafening explosions.

Twenty seconds passed, twenty-five, thirty, thirty-five, thirty-seven, and then ...

Chapter Nineteen

There was silence. Bartlett and McNeil exchanged glances, each feeling the slight shiver that reverberated through the ship's skeleton, and the hesitation, subtle as a missed heartbeat, that followed.

A second later, their fears were confirmed. The master panel suddenly filled with light, warning alarms broke the calm, and the sound of the engine room bell pierced the bridge with an urgency of its own.

The ship continued forward, now slowly turning to starboard as though she'd rubbed against something solid, causing her to veer in a different direction.

The captain snatched up the phone.

"Damn," he growled. Then, "Yes, I see. We'll be down in a minute."

The captain turned from the phone and punched a button on the console, acknowledging the alarms. Although the bridge was soundless again, red and yellow lights blinked furiously.

"Engines have stopped."

"My God." It was McNeil, finding his voice. "The watertight doors are starting to close, sir."

"Which bulkheads?" the captain asked.

"Forward bulkhead A ... B ..." McNeil began reciting as each red indicator light came on. "... C ... D ... E ... F ..." He paused. "No more at this point, sir."

Bartlett turned on his heel and bellowed an order to Geller. "Sound the emergency signal. For crew only."

"Yes, sir."

"I don't want any of the passengers alarmed until I know the extent of the damage." He directed his comment to everyone on the bridge. "Understand?"

Abram, Melika, and Clay had taken positions well out of the way. The three nodded. McNeil, Geller, and Pearce responded in unison with "Aye, aye, sir." Blair moved forward to assist on the bridge.

Janus stared at the dark ocean beyond the window. "This can't be," he said to himself. "This isn't right."

Geller jabbed the red emergency button. Immediately, the horns on the bridge and throughout the officers' spaces on the ship began sounding short blasts. After blaring eight times, there was one long blast, at which point Chief Officer Tannara bolted in through the rear bridge door. He was pulling his jacket over his pajama tops.

"Good, Hank, you're here," the captain said. "Boilers five and six have blown. It looks like we've got a tear in the hull from bulkhead F to the bow. I'm going below decks to assess the damage. You and Blair take over here. McNeil, come with me. Janus, you're coming, too."

McNeil hustled out the rear, portside door, the captain following. Janus didn't move. He was shaking his head, staring at the flashing amber and red lights, mesmerized. His eyes looked vacant and lost. The captain rushed back, grabbed Janus's arm, and dragged him outside.

"Come on," Melika said to Abram. "You know this ship as well as Janus. We need to get below."

"Okay," he said. He wanted to see what happened as well. "Stay here," Abram said to his father.

"You're damn right," Clay responded.

Abram and Melika hurried out the back door of the bridge, bumping into two officers rushing to their stations. Nobody slowed to offer apologies.

Melika didn't waste any time, moving as quickly as she could on the open deck.

Abram stayed with her as they jumped over the chain cordoning off the officers' deck from the passenger promenade and ran into the grand staircase entrance.

Biting the forefinger of her fist, Melika stopped at the top of the stairs. She said, "All the watertight doors in the forward bulkheads are closed."

"Yeah. A through F," Abram said.

Melika eyed the staircase. "Where are we in relation to bulkhead F?"

"It's the first bulkhead forward."

"Unbelievable. We're almost in the middle of the boat." She hurried down the stairs.

Abram didn't follow.

"Come on, Abram!" she yelled. Her voice carried up the empty stairs. The passengers were either in bed or enjoying the warmth of a lounge, unaware of the explosion in the *Sister*'s lower decks.

"Wait," he said.

"There isn't time."

"We can't take these stairs. We need to get ahead of bulkhead F because of the watertight doors."

"How?"

"If we can get down to the seamen's quarters, there's a staircase that'll get us to G deck."

"Fine. Where are we when we reach G deck?"

Abram rubbed his forehead, trying to picture the *Sister*'s layout in his head. "I think it's open like *Titanic*. Third-class berths."

Melika threw up her arms. "There is no third class on the *Sister*, Abram."

"I know. I'm not sure what's there. But it'll lead to the holds."

"All right. Let's go."

They retraced their steps to a set of stairs that serviced a ventilation shaft ahead of bulkhead F. They descended as far as Scotland Row, finding the door to the seamen's quarters on the starboard side near the entrance to the Harrods department store. As they approached, several seamen burst through. Abram grabbed the door before it closed, fearing it might lock.

"Better get back to your cabins," one of the seamen called to Abram. Instead, Abram and Melika entered the seamen's quarters without challenge amidst the chaos.

"The stairway is just ahead," Abram said.

Clambering down the metal stairs, they were about to head toward G deck when Abram held out his arm, blocking Melika's way.

"Wait," he said.

"What now?"

"Listen."

"Just a bunch of men yelling orders."

"No. Something else."

"Oh, boy. I hear it now."

"Look, I can see it."

Blue-green seawater rose in the stairwell. Like a whirlpool, it swirled underneath the stairs, the icy water forcing warm air out of its way.

From somewhere below they heard more rushing water, then the voices of frantic seamen. A series of crashes followed as the ocean ripped the walls and partitions like they were paper.

Abram pressed his ear against the forward wall. "Listen to this. There's water on the other side of this bulkhead. Probably over our heads. Let's get out of here."

"Right."

Running back up the steps, Melika lost her footing and started to tumble backwards. Abram caught her. Regaining her balance, she vocally cursed the man who invented tight dresses. Abram knew her near-fall had nothing to do with a restrictive wardrobe. *Titan's Sister* had already developed a list to starboard.

"Go back up to Scotland Row," he said, sticking close to Melika. "Then aft to the squash court. We'll see if there's damage there."

"Okay."

On F deck, they ran into a carpenter hurrying from baggage hold number two. He was soaked, his clothes clinging to his skin. He took the steps two at a time, dancing quickly around Abram and Melika in the narrow staircase, not stopping to answer their questions.

When they reached E deck, a young sailor burst through the door. He wasn't wet, but he was definitely shaken.

Abram slowed him down by stepping in his way. "How bad is it?"

The sailor shook his head. "We've lost boiler room number six to the rising water. Get topside."

"Jesus."

"What do you think?" Melika asked.

"Come on," Abram said.

They had to go up to get down with the bulkhead doors closed. Back on F deck, they rounded the corner to the lounge overlooking the squash courts. Abram ran to the windows and looked down.

Neither he nor Melika could immediately grasp the scope of what they were seeing. A few hours ago, they'd batted around a little green ball on these courts. Now, the water was claiming them. It wasn't churning or rushing in from the forward section. No, it was a quiet, steady advance—little ripples of water, rising gently up the squash court floor. The eerie calm belied the cold-blooded monster they'd met minutes before. But the sight was just as ominous. Like a cancer spreading silently through its host, the water was quietly consuming the ship, creeping up the squash court walls and floor, highlighting the increasing angle of the ship towards the bow.

Abram looked at his watch. Nearly midnight. "Melika," he said, taking a breath.

"Yes."

"We'd better get to our lifeboats."

"No," Melika said, turning from the window overlooking the squash court. "We can't be sinking."

One of the empty high-backed stools near the lounge's bar swiveled in response to the listing ship.

Ice melting in a glass crackled and shifted.

The lounge had closed only ten minutes ago. The waiter, Abram figured, had finished counting his evening's cash receipts and was about to tidy the tables when he saw water moving over the squash court floor. He had fled, leaving the bar as it was when the last customer had dropped a dollar tip on the table and staggered out the door.

Empty beer bottles littered the tables, as well as glasses and half-empty bowls of popcorn and nachos. Scattered around the room, soft leather chairs were either pushed together, affording their recent occupants greater intimacy, or turned toward the window for a view of the games below.

The smell of sweat from those who'd played hard-fought games clung to the air.

Abram touched the blood-crusted bruise he'd received from the fall in his bathroom. The wound was sore, the pain extending from his injury down his neck and into his stomach, where the anguish of a missed opportunity still fermented and bubbled.

He bent down behind the bar and pulled out two shot glasses, along with a bottle of Jim Beam. "Want a drink?"

Melika looked at Abram like he was nuts. "No. Where's your head?"

"You sure? It's free. The bartender forgot to lock up."

"It's stealing. Come on, let's get out of here."

"Melika, trust me. In a little over two hours, this ship's heading for the ocean floor. Have a drink. Claim salvage rights, if that'd make you feel better."

"It's not possible. Unless you know something I don't. Something about Janus. Something you and he are involved in."

Always the cop, Abram thought. "Believe what you want about me," he said. "It's over." Conceding his loss to whomever or whatever had caused this to happen, Abram lifted his glass and made the gesture for cheers, not in Melika's direction but at the water rising in the squash court. He sat on the stool behind the cash register and took a long sip of his drink.

Like a mother at wit's end, Melika put her hands on her hips. "This is no time for bourbon."

Abram chuckled, a throaty laugh. "Then you haven't heard the story of how one of the stewards saved himself from *Titanic*."

"How many of Clay's painkillers did you take?"

"Hear me out." He moved to the edge of the stool and propped his elbows on the bar, leaning toward Melika. "See, the steward was on deck, helping with the lifeboats. Every time he thought nobody would notice, he'd run down to his quarters and warm himself with stiff English whisky. By the time the ship sank, he was loaded. He swam over to one of the overturned lifeboats and hung to its side for six hours in the freezing water because there wasn't room to pull him aboard. When they got him on the rescue ship, all the medical attention he needed was something warm to drink."

"Folklore. Fifteen hundred people died within minutes in that frigid water. Besides, we have lifeboats for all."

Abram took another long pull on his drink. "You'll still need fortification."

"Yeah, and in the middle of the North Atlantic, bobbing around in one of those little lifeboats, with no hope of rescue for hours, I'd have to go pee."

"Oh. That would be awkward."

"Yeah, no kidding. Now, pull yourself together." She went to the door. "Are you coming?"

Instead, Abram finished his drink. Plunking the glass down on the counter, he got up from the bar stool to check on the rising water below. It was halfway up the squash court walls. "I'll make you a deal," he said without turning from the window. "If boiler room number five is taking on water, then we're getting off this ship, no questions asked."

"Fine. How do we get to boiler room number five?"

*   *   *   *

They returned to the mall, E deck, where the grand staircase ended. A less-elaborate stairwell, narrow but with a banister in the center, led to the deck below. Melika was halfway down, Abram still on the landing, when they heard a desperate voice.

"Wait. Wait."

Melika hesitated.

"It's Michael," Abram hollered.

"Michael? What on earth is he doing down here?"

The cabin boy was nearly falling down the stairs from the reception room above.

Melika quickly backtracked, reaching the landing just in time to catch the boy as he leaped from the last step. His momentum carried them into the ferns and hibiscus plants nestled near a fountain. The ship's angle caused the fountain's water to splash on the polished marble floor.

"Michael," she yelled, regaining her footing. "Are you crazy?"

He tried to catch his breath; his face was a blotchy red from exertion, and his hair was damp with sweat and matted to his blemished skin. A life jacket, strapped tight to his chest, covered a heavy wool sweater and a rumpled coat. "The flooding," he said, between breaths. "It's bad."

"Just take it easy. Slow down," Melika said. She gripped the boy's shoulders, leaning down to his level. "Everything's going to be okay."

He shook his head frantically. "The captain wants to talk to Mr. Harwood. Please," Michael said. "The ship's in trouble."

Abram took Melika's arm. "We've got to get the kid out of here."

She stood, moving away from Abram's touch. Michael grabbed her arm with both his hands and started tugging, forcing her to take a step. "Please, Ms. Jones."

She looked down at Michael. The boy swallowed hard.

He was still holding her arm, pulling her toward the stairs, when a crash came from below. A low rumble followed. Cold air vaulted up the steps. In its wake came an unnatural smell: a mix of salt water, diesel fuel, and grease. It was so heavy she could taste it, a rancid bile of destruction that lodged in her throat and starved her lungs of air.

Michael instinctively let go of Melika and jumped toward the stairs. His feet tangled as he turned.

Abram grabbed him, hustling him up the steps.

The rumble continued, echoing from every angle. It was a low, guttural sound that shook the floors and walls.

Melika peered down, expecting the area below to erupt with water. Instead, only a small rivulet ran down a closed door, playfully dodging the placard marked "For Crew's Use Only."

"Hurry!" Abram yelled.

The rivulet was broadening, flowing faster, joined by other streams coming from the top and sides of the door. Melika thought she heard a scream, then banging—two short raps—muffled but heavy.

It was crazy to open the door, but her duty as a cop was to save lives.

She hustled down the steps. Braced herself.

Before she could turn the knob, Abram grabbed her and dragged her back up. She tried to find her feet. Abram pushed her aside, a surprisingly hard blow to the chest that stole her wind and left her lying on the floor. She was quick to recover, yet not quick enough.

Abram was back down the stairs, his hand on the doorknob.

"Abram, no!" she yelled from the landing.

The stairwell exploded, a surge of white water blasting through the door, throwing him against the wall. The swell waned for only a moment before rising up again. Abram grabbed the only thing within reach: the doorknob. It was a small sphere of reprieve from the ultimate danger of being sucked under and dragged downstream by the unrelenting flow.

"Hang on!" Melika shouted, running into the icy water. Waist deep, she fought the pull of the racing ocean. Holding the last rung of the banister with a death grip, she yelled, "Grab my hand! Hurry."

Abram reached out, both of them struggling against the strong undercurrent that separated them.

"Come on, come on!" she shouted. "You can reach."

The water was rising, the sound of destruction deafening. With debris welling up under her, she wasn't even sure a floor was beneath her anymore.

"Just a few more inches," she yelled.

From the depths, something bumped Melika's leg, tugged at her dress, climbed up her back. She nearly screamed when a head appeared behind her, a man, squirming to save himself, wrapping his arms around her neck, and stealing all but the last of what air remained in her lungs. She yelled at him, not to get off, but to shift down her arm toward Abram and grab him so she could keep a solid hold on the banister's slippery rung.

The man didn't understand. She had no breath left to tell him again. Soon it wouldn't matter. The ocean was up to their shoulders, its force growing stronger.

There was another explosion. Water and debris raced through the doorway, ripping through the framing.

Melika watched as Abram pulled his arm from her. *He's giving up.* "Abram, no!" *Christ, there has to be another way.* She closed her eyes and loosened her grip on the banister. With arms wide, muscles stretched to the limit, she reached across the torrent. She was hanging on by her fingernails. "Abram, I'm here. Abram!"

She couldn't see him.

"No," she screamed, slapping the water's surface with her flattened hand.

Her fingers slipped from the banister's smooth surface, and she felt a jolt as the racing water took hold of her.

And somewhere in the icy rage, her arms still spread and the instinct to swim yet to kick in, she found Abram's hand.

But she wasn't being pulled downstream. She felt like she was being pulled apart, her arms tugged in different directions. Abram on one hand, something with a strong grip on the other, forcing her to make a choice—let go of one for the sake of the other. It wasn't going to be Abram. Not this time.

Melika took a deep breath and tried to wrench her other hand free.

"I could use a little help here," said a strange male voice. "At least stop trying to fight me."

The man Abram had saved … the guy who'd nearly choked the life out of her … had pulled himself up the staircase to safety and grabbed Melika by the wrist. Michael, that loveable, young kid, was holding the man's belt, an anchor for the human chain they'd formed.

With Melika's help, they pulled Abram clear of the water. On the landing, they tripped over each other, ending up in a pile.

Michael was quick to untangle himself. "I told you."

Melika blinked salt water from her eyes. *Yeah, and so did Abram.*

Chapter Twenty

At the back of the bridge, as he leaned over a table covered with the *Sister*'s deck plans, Abram pulled a blanket tighter around his body, fighting the shivers. Both he and Melika had changed into heavy seamen's fatigues, though even dry clothes weren't enough to fight the cold that had reached the marrow in their bones.

Melika had declined a blanket, saying that pacing would warm her up. But when an officer draped his jacket over her shoulders, she didn't argue.

It seemed like ages, Abram thought, since they'd been in the cruise line's terminal waiting to board the *Sister*. He'd offered her his windbreaker, and she'd refused with her typical obstinate look. Now, with her arms crossed tightly over her chest, her shoulders stiff and rounded, she looked more than just cold. She looked raw, exposed, as if this one layer of protective gear was all she had left, and she knew it wasn't going to be enough.

As for Abram's dad, Clay sat near the front window, rubbing his knees, watching the bow sink deeper and deeper into the water. Abram desperately wanted to tell Pop how sorry he was, that he'd never meant for this to happen, but Abram just didn't know what to say.

"Well, how bad is it?" the captain asked. He was on one side of Abram, Chief Officer Tannara on the other.

Abram focused once again on the newspaper-sized blueprints before him. He shuffled through them, looking for the one that might offer some insight into how—if—they could get out of this mess. Bartlett was calm, steady. Either he was relying on his naval training to set an example and not panic, or he was convinced the ship was not foundering.

"This one," Abram said, pulling out a longitudinal cross-section from the deck plans. It showed the *Sister* cut in two from bow to stern, detailing her skeleton—the outline of her hull, decks, and more importantly, the watertight bulkheads. They rose from the double bottom like twelve straight backbones. He pulled a chair to the table and picked up a pencil.

"The first three compartments," Abram said, attempting to illustrate the damage, "are open to the sea, and the pumps can't control the flooding. Correct?"

Bartlett nodded.

Abram put an X through each of the first three compartments. "I've seen the fourth compartment," he said. "By now, the squash court is probably full of water, and it's what, some thirty-two feet above the keel?"

"Right," Bartlett said.

Abram added another X. "I'm assuming because boiler six exploded, the fifth compartment is gone. And I nearly drowned in the sixth." He looked up. Melika had squeezed in between him and the captain, her jaw muscles twitching. Abram Xed out compartments five and six.

Melika returned to her pacing.

"What about further aft?" Abram asked the captain.

"The rest of the ship aft of bulkhead F is dry," Bartlett said.

Abram set the pencil down, shaking his head. "We both know that current shipbuilding regulations only require a vessel to stay afloat with two adjacent compartments flooded. Here we have the first six open to the sea."

"That's true, Mr. Harwood," the captain said. "But the *Sister* is no ordinary ship."

Abram considered this, tapping his pencil on the blueprint. "Janus knows the ship as well as I do. Where's he?"

Bartlett motioned to the back door. "He's in my cabin. Of no use, I'm afraid."

"Why? What happened?"

"He seems to be drifting in and out of reality. The doctor thinks the stress of our situation has triggered a mental breakdown. Janus just keeps saying that he should've listened. That he'd been warned."

"Warned?" Abram thought of the three messages he'd received.

"I don't know what he means. Warned," Captain Bartlett said. "Regardless, Ms. Jones was right. Janus admitted that he reprogrammed the ship's navigational computer soon after we set sail. He wanted us to reach *Titanic*'s SOS position, not her true position, at the time she foundered. A surprise out of the blue, just like *Titanic*'s iceberg."

"You didn't notice beforehand?"

"If you recall, our navigational system was down. At least, Janus made it appear that way. He blocked manual intervention and reprogrammed the tachometers so they indicated the speed we should've been going rather than what we actually were. I'm assuming that's possible."

Abram considered this. "I guess. Essentially, he put the ship on cruise control. But instead of setting a particular speed, he programmed a specific destination and time."

"Yes, by taking control of the automated guidance system. Is Janus smart enough to do that?"

Abram nodded. "Janus? Yeah, he'd know how to interface to the AGS." Abram lowered his eyebrows. "Although—"

"What?"

"The AGS capability is limited. Did Janus explain how he got the ship to mimic *Titanic*'s fatal maneuver around the iceberg?"

"No. That's when he started saying he'd been warned."

Melika had stopped her pacing and was standing behind them. She'd overheard them. "That son of a bitch sank us."

Bartlett shook his head. "It was the failure of the relief valves on boilers five and six that ultimately sank us—if we are sinking. Mr. Harwood?"

Abram looked at the blueprint once again. "If it were just the first four compartments flooded, we might stay afloat, though we'd never make it back to port on our own. But with six adjacent bulkheads flooded, there really doesn't seem to be much doubt."

"How much time do we have?" the captain asked.

Abram sat back. He let the blanket fall from his shoulders. "Two hours. Maybe three. The *Sister*'s structurally similar to *Titanic*. But she's lighter because the hull is welded, not riveted. So maybe we won't go down as fast."

Melika was quick to interject. "What about the cargo?"

Bartlett glanced over his shoulder. "We can't save the cargo, Ms. Jones."

"I'm more concerned about its weight."

"She's right," the captain said. "We are bow heavy."

"Damn." Abram made fists. "Is there no way to catch a break?"

"It would appear not." Bartlett turned to his fourth officer. "Geller, what ships are near?"

"There's nothing on radar, sir."

"All right." Bartlett motioned for his officers to gather around. Those who hadn't been on watch at the time of the explosion were now on the bridge. "Officer Graves," Bartlett said. "Start sending an SOS. Situation critical. Foundering imminent. And launch a communication buoy. If we sink before anyone can get to us, at least the buoy will continue to transmit our location."

"Yes, sir."

Bartlett nodded at Geller. "You'd better join him."

"Yes, sir."

"Tannara, you and Blair have the lifeboatsmen uncover their boats and provision them for evacuation. Keep the extent of the damage to within this group. I don't want the passengers stampeding. And I don't want our crew to panic. Just make sure they do the job as they were taught to do."

"Aye, aye, sir." Tannara and Blair saluted and left.

"Officer Jacobs, you'd better get Ms. Jones, Mr. Harwood, and Mr. Harwood's father some life jackets."

"Yes, sir."

"I'm going to put the passengers off in lifeboats," Bartlett said, taking a long look out the window, "and pray the weather holds. God be with them there. He certainly has abandoned us here."

Chapter Twenty-One

At 12:25, forty-five minutes after the boilers blew, Second Officer Blair reported to the captain that the lifeboats had been uncovered and swung out. The captain confirmed with his second officer that each boat had been provisioned with food, as well as a navigation kit including a compass and portable transmitter. They were ready, but Bartlett didn't call the passengers to the lifeboat stations.

"Officer Geller," Bartlett said.

"Yes, sir."

"Status of rescue vessels, please."

"Sir, the Canadian Coast Guard has responded with a cutter and a rescue ship."

"How long?"

"Six to eight hours, sir."

"Is there no one closer?"

"No, sir."

Bartlett turned to his sixth officer. "What's the temperature, Pearce?"

"Thirty degrees, sir, and falling. Wind's picking up."

The captain rubbed the back of his neck. "Six hours in a lifeboat in the middle of the North Atlantic can be as deadly as staying on a sinking ship." He looked up. "We've no choice. Sound the alarm. Everyone to their lifeboat stations."

Clay slipped off the stool he hadn't ventured far from all night and tightened his life jacket. Melika adjusted hers as well.

Abram turned his attention back to the *Sister*'s blueprints, brushing aside the life jacket an officer had left for him. He'd been staring at the *Sister*'s skeleton until the six Xs crossing out the forward compartments had blurred together. The circle Abram had made around the bulkhead separating the fifth and fourth compartments stood out like a mirage. It offered a sense of hope where none actually existed. Bulkhead F. Far higher than regulations required. With the watertight doors closed, Melika and Abram had been up and down decks all night trying to get around it. He thought it was part of *Titanic*'s design, though it sure was awkward on the *Sister*.

"Where's Blake's book?" Abram demanded.

"Whose book?" the captain asked.

"Blake Tellemann's."

Melika turned to Abram. "Why? What are you thinking?"

Abram closed his eyes, trying to concentrate. "I'm not sure. Just ... I need to check his book." He focused on the blueprint again.

"It's in your cabin." Melika turned quickly toward the door. "I'll get it."

The captain held his arm out, stopping her. "What deck?"

"Cabin B57," she said. "It won't be flooded. I'll be fine."

"You'll be drowned by the flood of people heading for the lifeboats." Still holding his arm in front of Melika, the captain yelled for one of his petty officers and pointed to the crew's stairs. "Get down to B57. We need a book called ..."

Melika hesitated.

"*The Great Sea Disaster of the North Atlantic,*" Abram said.

"Now!" the captain yelled. He turned to Abram.

"See how high this bulkhead goes?" Abram said.

"Bulkhead F? Yes?"

"With all the watertight doors closed in the bulkhead, it effectively cuts off the bow from the rest of the ship."

"I see that."

Abram tossed his pencil on the table and sat back, crossing his arms. "*Titanic* should *not* have sunk."

Melika and the captain spoke at the same time. "What?"

"So *we* won't sink?" Melika asked.

"I don't know," Abram said. "There might be some explanation in the book."

They didn't have long to wait. The petty officer was back in record time.

Abram leafed through the pages, finding *Titanic*'s bulkhead layout near the front. "This is interesting."

"What?" The captain moved closer.

"*Titanic*'s bulkhead F only goes as high as E deck. But look. Blake has hand-drawn a line extending the bulkhead to C deck. He and Janus must've decided on the change." Abram flipped back a few pages. "Just as I thought. According to the British inquiry, *Titanic* would've remained afloat if this bulkhead went as high as it does on the *Sister*." Abram looked up, hands pressed together as if in prayer. "Thank you, Blake," he whispered.

Captain Bartlett pointed to the critical bulkhead. "How do we know the explosions didn't damage it?"

Abram took a deep breath. "Good point." He sat back. Rubbing his chin, he said, "There's one other concern. After the *Sister*'s near-fatal launch, we did finite element analysis on the steel hull. Just to be sure the strain hadn't caused significant damage. It hadn't. Not for normal cruising. But we never considered an explosion of this magnitude. Small cracks in the welds may have been overlooked. That may explain why the hull opened up toward the bow."

"That being the case," the captain said. "I don't think I can count on bulkhead F."

"Maybe not. If it's damaged in any way, it might collapse trying to hold back so much water. Then we're right back where we started."

"Yes. And as you know, with the cargo we're carrying, the *Sister*'s being pulled down very quickly, putting more and more pressure on that bulkhead every minute."

Abram considered this. "What if we tried to equalize the pressure? Open all the watertight doors? Rather than the water pulling her down by the bow, she might settle on an even keel."

"Flood the rest of the ship?" the captain asked.

"It may not keep her afloat," Abram said, "but it'll give us some more time. It's either that or hope bulkhead F holds."

Bartlett pulled the blueprint closer. "Your plan's a little unorthodox, Mr. Harwood. The design of lateral bulkheads is to allow the water to flow from one side to the other, to keep the ship from tipping over. If we let it have free rein to flow from bow to stern, I can't predict what will happen."

"I know," Abram said.

Bartlett tapped his chin with his fist. "Officer Blair," he said.

"Yes, sir."

"Have the lifeboatsmen stand down."

"Yes, sir." Blair left by the aft door to relay the message.

"We'll count on the integrity of bulkhead F," the captain said. "But we'll prepare for the worst. If bulkhead F fails, I want all doors aft to be open so the ship can level off." The captain turned to his crew. "Can we open the doors from here?"

The first officer piped in. "Sir, they're all on manual override now. Someone is going to have to physically open each door."

"Notify the control room we're opening all doors abaft of bulkhead F. Then round up all the carpenters for the job. The engineers have their hands full right now. Have them work in teams of two. Start at the stern, working forward to bulkhead G." The men turned immediately to carry out their orders. "Remember," the captain yelled after them. "Under no circumstances is anyone to open the doors in F unless I give the order. And ... if it looks the least bit doubtful, tell them to get out of there immediately."

The first officer acknowledged the order and quickly left the bridge to find some hands.

Once again, the room was still.

"It's a lot to count on," Bartlett said. "How long until we know?"

"Well, the last report we got," Abram said, "water was thirty-five to forty feet above the double bottom in the compartment immediately forward of bulkhead F. If it holds, the water should stop rising within twenty minutes at the most."

Chief Officer Tannara returned to the bridge in time to catch the last of Abram's comments. The first officer was back as well.

"All right," Bartlett said to his men. "I'm delaying the launch of the lifeboats for now. We'll count on that bulkhead. But I want every man at the ready. If it collapses or is breached, evacuation is to commence immediately."

"Understood," Chief Officer Tannara acknowledged.

Bartlett once again looked at his watch, then left the bridge through the door to the starboard wing. A cold wisp of air reached into the room.

Without the captain's presence, the bridge was ominous, the red and yellow lights on the control panel continuing their baleful pulse.

It was a few minutes past twelve thirty. Whether the bulkhead held or not, they had a little while yet.

Abram got up and headed for the aft door, catching hold of Melika's arm as he passed. "Come on," he said. "I need your help."

Chapter Twenty-Two

When they stepped onto the boat deck, neither Abram nor Melika was able to fully comprehend what they faced.

People were scattered around the deck, unsure of where they should be or what they should be doing. Sailors stood by the boats, shouting, cupping their hands to their mouths, and attempting to organize the passengers. But their voices were lost in the noise of the screeching ship as she blew off steam from the boilers below.

Abram pushed through the people with Melika close behind.

Then suddenly the thunderous voice of the ship died. In its absence, a noise just as unnerving filled the void. Silence. The last of the *Sister*'s steam evaporated in the cold night.

Abram saw something he had never expected to see. All the lights on the deckhouses were ablaze, as well as her sidelights, the mast lights, the spots that highlighted her four towering funnels, and even the decorator lights that were strung the length of the hull. Obviously, the captain wanted rescue ships to see his vessel, and it afforded a tremendous amount of illumination for a safe evacuation. But it sent the wrong message. It was as if the open decks had been prepared for an after-dinner gala, a party to pay tribute to *Titanic*, just as Janus had wanted.

The horrendous noise of the ship had been a fearful sound. Now that it had stopped, more people were coming out on deck, joking with each other and tugging halfheartedly at the straps of their life jackets.

Some teenage girls giggled to each other about how they looked. A group of boys chased each other down the deck, dodging the lifeboat falls strung across the deck. Abram had to step aside so a group of card players could survey the situation with their drinks in hand. Near the entrance to the gymnasium, the smoking room's late-night band started to play.

For a moment, the illusion of safety even captured Abram. Knowing the strength of the steel he had welded together to fabricate the double bottom, the hull, the bulkheads, and each span that separated one deck from the other, he wondered how a ship of this size—of this length and breadth—given the most advanced safety features, could possibly sink. With the bright lights and cheerful music in the air, why would anyone dare to step off this ship into a little boat with no amenities of any kind? Despite the ship's growing list, it was hard to imagine that a lifeboat—a wood and fiberglass vessel, hundreds of miles from land—could be safer than the deck of this massive ship.

One of the card players approached Abram. His bow tie dangled from his neck, the top two buttons of his shirt were undone, and his cummerbund was loose and pulled slightly to one side. He tripped over Melika's feet and nearly spilled his champagne down Abram's front.

"Isn't this terrific?" the unkempt man slurred. "It's like fireworks on the Fourth of July."

Knowing it would be useless to try to convince the man of anything different, Abram stepped away, but the drunken man grabbed Abram's arm and tried to show Abram his watch.

"Look at the time," the man said. His grip was strong, suggesting he was using Abram more for support than anything else. Abram pulled away, disgusted by the heavy combination of bourbon and champagne on the man's breath.

"You're missing all the fun," the man said. "Don't you get it? It's the coup de grâce of the cruise."

"Come on," Abram said to Melika, pushing the man aside.

"Where are we going?"

"Trust me."

Melika followed as Abram hurried down the grand staircase, hoping to go down as far as C deck, then head aft.

As they moved steadily downward, they had to cling to the brass rail, fighting the ever-increasing number of people heading up. Some were climbing the steps two at a time, making light of the call to lifeboat stations. Some were taking the steps with frustrated measure, either carrying their sleepy children or lugging valuables and keepsakes they feared would be stolen if left behind. Then there were those who merely dragged themselves forward, some in their pajamas, others without shoes or shirts, whatever clothes they had soaking wet and sticking to their bodies.

Abram grabbed Melika's wrist when they reached B deck and pulled her out of the stream of people into a less congested hallway. They headed toward the stern, dodging people who stubbornly tried to close and lock their cabin doors. The ship's framing had shifted ever so slightly—the precision fit Abram's crew had been so careful to weld was now subject to the nearly unbearable stress of water consuming her hull. He was reminded of the launch, when he'd worried she'd split in two. Now the same fear grew in his stomach, but this time, the lives of hundreds of people were at stake.

After hustling through the doorway to the less elaborate aft grand staircase, Abram and Melika resumed their trek down to the lower decks, Abram moving faster because these stairs weren't nearly as crowded as those at the bow.

When they reached E deck, not a soul was in sight.

Abram stopped. "Okay, here's the plan," he said between breaths. "People are going to need coats, boots, whatever, to stay warm."

"Macy's?"

"Exactly. It's at the stern of the ship. It'll be dry. We'll make as many trips as we can."

Melika followed him quickly.

At the entrance to Macy's, surveying its huge, sliding glass door, Abram realized he hadn't anticipated it being closed. Melika pulled a lock pick from her pocket. "I can't get the damn thing open," she muttered, working at the lock.

Abram assessed the doors. They were twenty feet high, as wide as Scotland Row. "What if we tried to break the glass? With a garbage can or something?"

"The door's half an inch thick." She went back at it with her lock pick.

"Doomed from the beginning," Abram said, more to himself than to her.

Melika nodded.

An affront to powers yet to be understood, he thought. Fate's hand. The ship faltering in the launching way, the dock fire, the boilers coming on line, the locked relief valves ... He shook his head. "If one thing had been different."

Melika chuckled. "Yeah, just one thing. Easier said than done." She stood up again and stared at him through narrowed eyes, as if looking deep inside him. "It's not your fault, Abram."

He eyed her suspiciously. "You don't believe that."

"I'm not sure what to believe anymore."

"So you don't think I'm responsible for ... for all this?" He raised his hands, indicating the ship, the disaster.

"I meant something else."

"I think we should focus on the lock," he said.

Melika ran her hands down her face, inhaling as she did so. As she exhaled, she shook out her fingers, like a diver loosening up.

"Listen to me," she said.

"Why?"

She cleared her throat. "There's something else. Something you should know."

"Make it quick."

"In your cabin. You said you owed Blake."

Abram didn't think she'd heard—or more accurately, understood—anything he'd said in his cabin.

"But," she said, "you don't know the whole story." She paused. Finally, she started to explain, her voice steady and soft. "Janus found Blake the morning of the launch. He didn't tell anybody because he didn't want the launch delayed."

"What?"

"Janus thought Blake was dead. So he didn't think it would matter."

Abram couldn't find words.

"I know you blamed yourself," she said, "for not getting on the ship earlier. But it wasn't your fault."

"Janus knew where he was?"

"Yes."

"He could've saved him?"

"Yes. He could've."

"That son of a bitch. I'll kill him. I swear." Abram quickly turned away. He squeezed his eyes shut and ground his teeth. He looked back, not at Melika, but at Macy's impenetrable door, one more frustration the world saw fit to hand him. He saw his own face, a distinct image in the solid glass. In lieu of Janus, he punched his reflection, two, three times, knowing it was useless.

"It's open," Melika said.

"What?"

Melika lightly rested her hand on his shoulder. "Can I ask you something?" she said. In the midst of the world's assault, her voice was calm, understanding, and empathetic. Disarming.

"Melika, please ..."

Her fingers touched his face. "Look at me," she said.

He did.

"I need to know something."

"I don't have answers to your questions."

"In the stairwell," she said. "Why didn't you leave it to me to save that guy on the other side of the door? Why'd you risk your life instead?"

He hoped to sound as steady and straightforward as his words. "I opened the door so you wouldn't have to."

From below, a foreboding voice, deep and bellowing, resonated throughout the ship and shook the floor and the glass wall in front of them.

No doubt the nearly one-foot thick, reinforced steel bulkhead had succumbed to the weight of two hundred thirty thousand cubic feet of water. Had they not been waiting for it, praying the bulkhead wouldn't fail, perhaps they wouldn't have noticed the momentary vibration of the ship and the low, deep-seated noise of rushing water that followed.

Goose bumps formed on Abram's arms. The icy ocean was making headway through the ship, a wave of cold air preceding it. The bulkhead was gone, and there was little time, no hope except to get off the ship and pray for luck. He checked over his shoulder. It wouldn't have surprised him to see water rushing down the hall toward them.

"Maybe they got the bulkhead doors open," Melika said.

"No. We'd be settling on an even keel already."

"How much time you figure we've got?"

"An hour and a half, maybe."

"Let's get what we came for and get out of here." Melika pushed open the glass door and hurried inside Macy's. "Come on. We gotta stick together."

Chapter Twenty-Three

The siren blared. Orders to abandon ship filled the night. This was not a drill, the intercom repeated. Everyone was to be at his or her lifeboat station.

Laden with coats, boots, mittens, sweaters, and scarves, Abram and Melika hurried up to the boat deck.

"Here," Abram said when they reached the open promenade, "you hand out the clothes. I'll get Pop."

"Abram, look!" Melika was staring down the deck at the lifeboat stations.

Abram dropped his armful of winter gear. "Shit, now what?"

The first set of lifeboats was loaded, but they still hung in the davits, level with the deck.

"Mr. Harwood!"

Abram turned, locating Second Officer Blair at station number seven.

"We need your help," Blair yelled.

Abram glanced at Melika.

"You go," she said. "I'll get your father."

Melika disappeared toward the bridge while Abram cut through the crowd to number seven.

The lifeboat was swaying back and forth. The senior lifeboatsman, a big, burly guy named Hawkins, was shouting at the passengers to stay in their seats. His partner, Gates, was helping a group of sailors clear the lines.

"The automation system has failed," Blair shouted, shoving a chock out of the way and wiping his forehead. "And now the winches are jammed. Tannara's got the same problem on the port side."

"What? You mean we have to launch manually?"

"Yes, and we're short hands. Can you work the rigging?"

Abram knew nothing about launching a lifeboat, but he grabbed the ropes at the stern. Hawkins had the bow's lines.

"All right, men, here we go," Blair said.

Blair and Gates simultaneously unlocked the tackle.

The rope jumped as it started through the blocks. Abram held on. Blair was quickly at his side, with Gates assisting Hawkins.

"Slow and easy now," Blair commanded. "Keep it level."

They started to let out the fall lines. The lifeboat inched down the side of the ship.

"Slower at the stern," a sailor said, watching the boat. "Steady …"

Abram was already sweating. Worried passengers in the lifeboat cried out in surprise as the front dipped, then the back, Blair's makeshift launch crew attempting to let the ropes out at a consistent speed.

"Almost there," the sailor reported.

Abram's arm muscles were aching. The blocks were designed to take most of the weight of the lifeboat. But even with Blair's help, it was difficult to keep the lines from racing through the pulleys. When the lifeboat finally landed in the water and the lines suddenly slackened, Abram nearly fell backwards.

Blair dropped the ropes and ran to the side. "Unhook the blocks," he yelled to the sailors in the lifeboat.

"What?" came a voice from the darkness below.

"The blocks. We've got to reel in the ropes to launch another boat. Hurry, there's no time to waste."

"Hold on. I can't see."

"Christ," Hawkins muttered. "Those idiots went down without a light."

Blair shouted over the side. "There's a flash in the provisions."

Abram pulled off his jacket and checked his watch again. It was 12:45. At this rate, they wouldn't get everyone away. "Are we launching all of them?" he asked, pointing to the lifeboat mounted on deck and the other boat nested above.

"No," the second officer replied. "Two per station. Then we move on."

Abram glanced at the bottom boat mislabeled *Titanic*. "Good," he said.

"Sailor," Blair yelled, "what's the problem with the blocks?"

"I've got it," was the response. "Haul 'em up."

"Jesus, this is going to take forever," Hawkins mumbled, pulling hard at the ropes, elbowing a passenger and nearly knocking him over.

People were everywhere, tripping over the ropes and demanding explanations while the crew struggled to clear the lines.

"This is a joke, right?" one of the passengers yelled. "Part of the *Titanic* experience?"

"Get to your station," Blair said. "This isn't a drill." But the passengers didn't want to believe what now seemed obvious, and Blair turned from them, frustrated, his attention focused again on launching the second boat.

"Swing the davits back," he ordered once they'd reeled in the fall lines.

Gates tried the forward hand wheel. "I can't get them to budge."

Abram struggled with the aft hand wheel. "They're just stiff," he said between clenched teeth.

With two men at each hand wheel, they managed to swing the davits into place. Hawkins and Blair climbed up to secure the blocks to the next lifeboat.

Blair attempted to snap the stern pulley into place. "Give me slack."

"Got it at the bow," Hawkins shouted, jumping back on deck.

"Right, let's get them back out," Blair ordered when he was ready.

The lifeboat gradually swung over the side as the men struggled once again with the hand wheels.

"Okay, level it up with the deck," Blair said. "Good. Now, lock off the fall lines and load up the passengers."

A steward had managed to organize a group of forty or so people.

With one foot on the gunwale of the lifeboat and his other foot on *Titan's Sister*, Abram helped the passengers step from the deck of the ship into the stern of the small boat.

"Anyone else?" he heard Hawkins yell after the passengers were in.

No one came forward.

"Lower away," Blair shouted.

It was shortly after 1:00 AM. A crewman reported that the lifeboats at stations three and five had also set sail. On the port side, progress was slower, with only the boats at stations six and eight launched.

By now, the *Sister* had gently rolled in the water, her list changing from starboard to port while the bow sank deeper.

They worked faster.

At one point, Hawkins suggested lowering the lifeboats to A deck to take on passengers there because of the lack of room on the boat deck. But getting people to board through the windows of the enclosed promenade would delay progress even further. Gates proposed launching the boats partially filled then having them row to the gangway doors to pick up the remaining passengers. But by the time they got everyone organized to head below, the doors were underwater.

So they continued to toil from the boat deck, Hawkins cursing the remaining lifeboats.

They were lowering a boat at station seven when Abram realized that the reception area on D deck—the grand staircase where they'd boarded the *Sister*—was flooded. Water was gushing through one of its portholes, threatening to swamp the lifeboat.

Ten minutes later, a passenger pushing others aside yelled that *Titan's Sister*'s name was gone, and at 1:40, a crewman reported that the forward well deck was awash and the bow's forecastle deck was an island, disconnected from the deckhouses by a canal of shallow water.

Blair looked desperate. They still had the second boats at stations thirteen and fifteen, as well as the boats at station number one, to load and lower.

As the water rose faster, progress slowed on her decks. People were frantic now. Some who'd missed their assigned boats were screaming at the top of their lungs that they were about to die. One man grabbed Hawkins's arm as he was securing the blocks for lowering and nearly sent the lifeboat crashing into the crowd. Others were refusing to board the boats until they had assurances that their friends and loved ones wouldn't be left behind. Blair confirmed there were lifeboats for all.

They got the remainder of the aft boats away and were racing forward to launch the boats at station one when Abram noticed the first trickle of water on the boat deck. The water hadn't climbed up the front of the deckhouses yet. Rather, the ocean had flooded the crew's forward staircase from below.

He wondered about Melika. She'd have seen his father off ages ago, but her cop instincts might've kept her on board to the last.

He quickly looked around. There were so many people in the way, none of them Melika.

"Either help or get off," Hawkins snapped at Abram.

Abram grabbed a rope and got back to work. The passengers pushed their way into the boat.

The second boat at station one went out relatively quickly despite the *Sister*'s increasing list to port. As they lowered it, the boat bumped and scraped the side of the ship. Abram heard Hawkins mutter a thank you under his breath to the men who'd welded the ship together. If the steel plates had been riveted like older vessels, the lifeboat would keep catching on the hull, likely tipping its contents into the sea.

All lifeboats on the starboard side, except for those mounted on deck, had now been launched. Passengers who'd missed taking their assigned seats had moved to the port side. The starboard deck was deserted and quiet.

It was almost 2:00 AM. Abram heard water gurgling up the forward hatch from number one hold. It swirled across the forecastle deck, pulling the ship lower. Within seconds, the deck was completely submerged, the bow gone. Now the ocean had less than twenty feet to climb before it would swirl around their ankles on the boat deck.

Abram, Blair, Hawkins, and Gates hurried to the port side to assist. Things weren't going as well there. With the ship listing heavily, loading the boats on this side was difficult and dangerous.

Abram stopped short of the crowd around stations two and four, and he peered down the length of the ship for Melika. He couldn't see her. But near the end of the boat deck, a group of people struggled with the second lifeboat at station fourteen. Except for those in the two forward stations, this was the last to go. Abram grabbed Gates and ran to the boat.

They pushed through the anxious group of people, Abram searching for Melika as he and Gates grabbed the hand wheels and swung the boat over the side. Someone snatched up nearby deck chairs. As they leveled the craft as best they could, the chairs were laid across the rail to bridge the gap between the ship and the dangling lifeboat. Abram locked the rigging and jumped over the ropes to the waiting passengers. Gates was in the lifeboat ready to grab the people as Abram helped them in.

As Abram took the closest woman by the hand, a throng of people surged forward, knocking into Abram and throwing the woman aside. Somewhere in the confusion, he heard a gunshot. He wasn't sure of the source. A second shot rang out, closer now, piercing his ears. As the people backed away, he saw

Melika. She was attempting to stay the crowd by firing her gun in the air.

"Quickly, but orderly. Everyone has a seat," she was yelling. "Don't end up dead in it."

Michael was standing beside her.

"Thank God," Abram whispered and quickly returned to loading the boat.

The line of people never seemed to end as Abram handed one person then another to Gates. The lifeboat kept drifting from the side of the ship with the ever-increasing list to port. Finally, it was time for Melika and Michael.

Abram took Michael's hand, helping the boy around the ropes. Gates reached out. Abram steadied himself with one foot on the deck chair. He didn't notice how much the gap between the ship and the lifeboat had increased during the loading.

Michael took a step forward, keeping his balance by using Abram's arm. Michael was about to jump when the chair slipped from the boat.

Abram lunged forward, grabbing Michael's wrist as the boy fell over the side, his weight pulling Abram toward the edge. Knowing they were both headed for the cold sea, Abram desperately swept the deck with his free arm, his hand finding a rail post, his fingers grabbing it. With a sudden stop, Michael's body banged into the side of the ship. The boy didn't scream as he struggled to get some sort of a hand- or foothold. The strain on Abram's arms and shoulders stole his breath and sent lightning bolts of pain through his upper body.

The lifeboat was swaying, a man inside reaching futilely for Michael's hand.

Abram heard someone yell, "Stay still. For Christ's sake, don't move, or you'll tip the lot of us."

"Jesus Christ, Abram," Melika yelled from the edge of the ship's deck. "Hold on."

Out of the corner of his eye, Abram saw Melika stretching to reach Michael.

Abram tried to pull himself up, or at least lift Michael so Melika could grab him.

"Come on, Abram, you can do it," Melika shouted.

He was trying. Damn it, he thought, gritting his teeth, he *was* trying. But Michael's movement to reach Melika was tearing through Abram's shoulder, the socket straining to hold his weight as well as Michael's.

Melika began yelling for someone to help. No one was in sight.

Throwing the fall lines from the deck into the lifeboat, she yelled to Gates. "Get ready," she said. "I'm going to unlock the rigging."

Abram grimaced. He knew what Melika was intending to do. Right now, Michael was lower than the lifeboat. Abram couldn't lift Michael into it. But if they lowered the boat to Michael's feet, perhaps Abram could swing the boy over and drop him in.

Did Abram have the strength?

Not if they didn't hurry.

The lifeboat dropped suddenly. He heard screaming, and then the boat stopped as quickly as it started.

"Damn it," he heard Melika say.

As Abram fought tears of pain in his eyes, he guessed what had happened. Despite the counterweight effect of the block and tackle at each end of the boat, the passengers who'd volunteered to work the falls weren't ready. The rope had raced through their hands before they could get a grip. The centrifugal clutch in the block grabbed the falls and stopped the boat from plunging into the ocean.

"Damn it," Melika shouted. "I can't loosen the ropes. They're jammed."

"Shoot the blocks!" Gates yelled.

"I can't. They're in line with the boat."

"Then throw me the gun."

Abram shut his eyes, anticipating the noise as he struggled to hold Michael.

He heard two shots, then Gates cursing, then another shot.

The blocks that clutched the rope weren't that far away.

Another shot.

Abram wondered how many rounds were in the gun.

It didn't really seem to matter now. Even if he could muster the physical strength, Abram's mind wasn't going to hold on. He was dizzy. Melika ... Michael ... Gates ... they were fading. The darkness took hold of them, stole them and everyone else in the crowded lifeboat, leaving nothing except empty seats.

Soon, Abram saw people climbing in. He didn't know them, but he recognized them. People from the past. Women and children. They moved quickly, unceremoniously. Some in hats and muffs, others draped in blankets, all wearing white life belts made of cork.

Hundreds from third class appeared on deck. They ran to the lifeboat, fearful of an officer with his gun, yet pushing toward him anyway, pleading to be told where their boats were, how they could save themselves. The men were held in check, while a handful of women and children clambered into the lifeboat. Most refused to leave their families, screaming and crying at the injustice, while the boat was lowered with plenty of room to spare.

A man, barely in his twenties, yelled above the frantic crowd.

"Please, I beg you," he said in a heavy accent. "My wife left in another boat. I owe it to her to save myself. Without me there is no one to take care of her or my infant son."

"Any more women and children?" was the cry as the boat started to lower.

The young man turned and ran to the other side of the ship. Abram prayed the fellow would have better luck there.

Soon Abram heard deck chairs—no, not just chairs—splash in the water.

Screams of agony, fear, hopelessness. A gunshot.

Ropes squeaked through pulleys. The shouts louder and more distinct.

"Swing him over."

"Come on, Abram, you can do it!" It was Melika.

Not desperate passengers. Not *Titanic*.

"Swing Michael over to the lifeboat."

If he could just save Michael.

Abram heard a man yell. "Hurry up. The ass end of this tub is getting higher and higher in the air by the second."

Abram couldn't feel his body. He didn't know how to tell his muscles to move when they didn't seem to be there anymore. He was numb. He was tired.

Melika kept shouting. "Abram, listen to me. You were right."

How could any of that matter anymore?

"I get it now," she said. "I was scared. Scared of getting too close."

Another man. Not as loud, not speaking in Abram's direction. "Jesus, lady. Now's not the time."

"Just shut up." Melika's voice. Always strong. "Abram, I'm still scared. Even more. Do you understand? I'm scared of losing you."

"Melika?"

"Yes, I'm here. You can do it."

Abram concentrated on his arm. He was telling it to move, but he wasn't sure it was responding.

The man again. "We're going to have to leave them."

As Abram registered these words, he sensed Melika moving beside him. He heard a collective gasp from the people in the lifeboat. She was over the side of the ship, clinging to a rope, moving toward Abram and Michael with a series of small jumps as if she were rappelling down a mountain. Michael grabbed her around the neck. With a loud grunt, she pushed herself from the hull of *Titan's Sister* and landed safely in the lifeboat.

Without Michael's weight, Abram felt as though he were floating.

"Can you pull yourself up?" Melika shouted.

He didn't use any of his precious strength to answer but swung his arm over his head and grabbed the rail. For a moment, he just hung there. Then he took a deep breath and managed to drag himself back on board.

"Abram!"

He turned to the lifeboat, his body still numb. "Go ahead," he shouted. "I still may be needed here." He tried to sound upbeat and unscathed.

"No, Abram," Melika said, but her boat was already disappearing into the inky darkness.

Hoping to find another way off the ship, Abram moved forward, working his muscles to feel them again. The deck was empty except for the lifeboats marked with *Titanic*'s name.

They sat on their supports ready to be attached to the davits. Yet Abram knew he couldn't drop a boat into the water by himself.

From the ocean's surface, the voices of the ship's forsaken passengers reached him. He couldn't make out their words, although it was clear they were trying to move as far away from the *Sister* as possible.

Abram rubbed his arms, beginning to feel the cold. He didn't even have a life vest.

He squinted, trying to spot any activity near station number two or four, where he'd left Blair and Hawkins. He didn't see anyone.

For a second, Abram merely listened to *Titan's Sister*. She was no longer struggling against her death. Abram heard a low moan from below as the water steadily moved through her shell. There was a soft whistle as the air was taken from her. There were no explosions, no ripping or tearing of metal, no crashing sounds of any kind. *Elegant to the end.*

He checked his footing and ventured down the length of the sloping boat deck. She had leveled out from port to starboard, but her list toward the bow was increasing. Maybe he should simply walk into the water rather than subject his body to the shock of jumping from the rail. Regardless, if he didn't reach a lifeboat within minutes, he'd be dead.

As he moved forward, he heard voices. With relief, he spotted their source after he was clear of the aft davits.

The lifeboat at station two, the last of the *Sister*'s lifeboats, was ready to be lowered with Blair, Hawkins, and Captain Bartlett. A handful of tired-looking men from the crew had already taken their seats.

Abram hurried down the deck and found a place in the bow of the little craft. Hawkins and Blair followed. Captain Bartlett was the last, taking one quick glance over his shoulder before his foot left the deck.

The crew let out the lines, the ropes creaking through the blocks. The lifeboat eased down the side of the ship. Light escaped from the portholes and reflected off the ocean's surface.

They were level with C deck, almost to the water, when a sweeping shaft of light caught Abram's eye.

He looked up. "Whoa, hold it. There's someone left on board."

Chapter Twenty-Four

Abram shifted to the far side of the lifeboat, leaning back to see the ship's upper decks. "I think it's Spin. The guy from the shipyard fire."

"Who?" the captain asked.

"Up there. On the roof."

Bartlett shook his head. "We didn't leave anybody." He stood to look anyway. "Where?"

Abram pointed to the area over the bridge and officer quarters. The man disappeared behind a cowl vent. "He was right there."

"Impossible," the captain said and motioned for his crewmen to cast off.

Abram knew what he saw. "I gotta go back. I gotta get on board." He grabbed the nearest fall line, counting on adrenaline for strength.

A sailor caught Abram's pant leg, but Abram pulled away. He hustled up the rope until he was able to roll over the ship's rail and back onto the *Sister*'s deck.

She was now perhaps fifteen degrees down by her bow. Incredibly, her emergency lights still shone, and in that weak luminance, Abram could see the forward mast. Its crow's nest, once towering above the ship, was just feet above the ocean's surface. Surrounded by water, isolated from the rest of the ship, it was a forlorn and weary testament, a symbol of man's fallibility.

"Is anyone on board?" Abram yelled.

No response.

"Is someone on the roof?"

Again no response—except from the *Sister*. She moaned, a distant, pathetic sound. Seconds later, she drifted forward and slightly to port, bracing herself for the final onslaught of the sea.

Abram took a deep breath. Bartlett was right. It was stupid to think someone would stay aboard.

But what if they couldn't leave? Maybe they were hurt or trapped. Like Blake the day of the launch.

If Abram had found Blake, if Janus hadn't left him to die …

The captain's voice rose from below. "Harwood, for Christ's sake, I checked that area myself. Now get your dumb ass down here."

Abram hesitated. He was sure he'd seen someone. But he reminded himself of how many times he'd said that before. Finally, he took hold of the rope to drop back into the lifeboat.

He was about to turn away when he saw another sweep of light.

"Damn it," he said. "I'm not going crazy."

A maintenance ladder was at the back of the deckhouse. Abram headed aft, dodging wooden chairs and fall lines. He scrambled up to the roof.

At the forward end was the man Abram had spotted. He held a flashlight under his arm while trying to unhook the tie-downs for the starboard's collapsible lifeboat.

"For Christ's sake, leave it." Abram yelled. His voice died in a series of muffled explosions from deep within the ship. They were hollow, reverberating sounds that shook the hull and caused her lights to flicker.

"Oh, shit." Abram steadied himself with the rail.

A prolonged, mechanical howl followed, the lower decks twisting between their steel supports and the guts of the *Sister* wrenching as the ocean's salty bile rose inside her. Air hissed through the vents as water poured into the space below, claiming another bulkhead compartment. In the midst of that, Abram could hear the quiet, ominous sound of water creeping up the face of the deckhouse, wooden chairs and debris banging into the promenade walls.

Determined to free both collapsibles from the roof, the man hustled to the port side.

Abram hurried forward, tripping over a cable stay but remaining on his feet. He grabbed the man's shoulder, intending to pull him away from the lifeboat. The man spun around, jerking himself loose. Before Abram had a chance to react, the guy yanked back his coat, pulled a gun from his belt, and aimed it straight at Abram.

"Women and children only," Janus said.

"Janus? Okay, okay," Abram said, raising his hands. "Just take it easy." He stepped back. "Everyone's gone. It's just you and me."

Janus kept the gun on Abram. With his other arm, he pointed toward the stern, at what little remained of his treasured ship. "So many people left to die. I can do no more. Can't you see?"

Yes, I can see. The tragic flaw of man, of Janus. Tempting fate with a twin of man's blatant arrogance: the mighty Titanic.

Unsinkable. Meaningless words in the face of nature's incalculable power.

"Can't you see them?" Janus demanded, pushing the gun closer to Abram.

Abram thought of the three men. Harbingers of disaster, messengers of fate. Had Janus seen them, too? Had they driven him mad? He had no time to play psychologist.

Somewhere below, the ocean broke loose, smashing through more bulkheads and rushing aft. The ship lurched forward. Abram grabbed the rail as a wave of water hit the bridge and swept across the roof, ripping the collapsible from its chocks and throwing it onto the deck below.

A shot skimmed past Abram's head. Instinctively, he ducked.

Janus, on his knees, fired wildly. "I'll shoot any man who gets near this boat."

Abram believed him and fought the impulse to run aft, to stay ahead of the advancing water.

Janus was back on his feet. He was yelling at someone, someone who wasn't there, and as he turned to fire in that direction, Abram jumped him.

The gun fell to the deck and slid toward the water. Janus scrambled forward. Landing on his stomach, he caught the gun with his fingertips just as a loud gushing sound erupted directly in front of them. The ocean swallowed the fore part of the bridge. Water swirled around the base of the forward funnel. It poured down the large ventilation shaft on the roof and rose steadily up the promenade below.

Janus struggled to get a solid grip on the gun. Abram tried to kick it away with his foot, but the ship shuddered, the weight of the water in her forward compartments pulling her down while the stern rose higher. They had only seconds left.

Abram locked his arm around the rail. He grabbed Janus by the collar and headed aft, but *Titan's Sister* had reached an angle her hull could no longer withstand. Her bow was buckling, and as the forward expansion joints opened wider under the strain, the lines tethering the first funnel to the ship snapped. Amid a shower of sparks, the circle of steel fell from its base and crashed into the water. Abram slipped, falling onto Janus. The gun went off.

A millisecond was all it took for Abram to realize that he hadn't been shot. But Janus cried out in agony, clutching his side. Abram grabbed the gun, though it was the least of his worries now.

The ocean was at their feet, pushing them back as though the ship were traveling forward. Dragging Janus, Abram couldn't stay ahead of it. A surge of water washed them off the roof and onto the lower roof of the first-class lounge. The ship's angle was close to thirty degrees, a nearly insurmountable pitch. Abram's boots slipped on the wet surface. Janus was in the water, holding out his hand. It would have been so easy to leave him. Leave him for dead, like he'd left Blake.

But Abram managed to get a footing and take hold of Janus, dragging him toward the stern again. At the steps heading down to the aft section of the boat deck, Abram could see the remaining lifeboats clinging to their supports.

"Thank God," he whispered.

A grinding, tearing sound filled the night. The ship's lights flickered then went out. Abram was blind. He couldn't even see the edge of the ship. By feel, he made his way down the steps to the boat deck.

Janus, breathing heavily but moving with renewed energy, pulled his flashlight from his pocket and focused the beam toward the stern. The chocks for the lifeboats were collapsing and breaking loose.

"Look out!" Abram jumped toward the deckhouse, but he couldn't get Janus out of the way. The lifeboats, *Titanic*'s lifeboats, one after the other, skidded down the promenade toward the water, crashing into Janus and sweeping him off the deck.

A great roar came from below. Everything from the ship's huge boilers to the cutlery placed for breakfast was tumbling toward the bow. A piercing sound rose around Abram. The moaning of the shifting decks had turned to a horrendous scream. The ship was breaking up under his feet. It was too late for Janus. In a few seconds, the suction would drag Abram under as well.

He grabbed anything solid to pull himself toward the stern. Door handles, rails, bolted-down benches. He was as far back as he could go on the boat deck when the ship seemed to pause.

Abram clung to the rail as the stern settled back. The ship had split apart, the night suddenly quiet.

Taking a breath, Abram listened. What was that sound? Then he realized what it must be. Rather than drifting away from the deadly scene, the empty lifeboats had clung to the side of the ship. They were bumping up against the hull in the midst of a gray, smoky vapor that rose from the water's surface. It grew thicker, climbing the deck, gaining momentum, making the boats disappear, the dense fog taking on shapes. The entire deck came alive, *Titanic*'s fifteen hundred souls either rushing to the stern, prolonging the inevitable, or screaming in the water for help that wouldn't come.

The cruel reality of the past had taken Janus. Now it had come back for Abram.

He was too tired to question it. Too tired to fight it.

He simply stepped mechanically toward the deadly cold sea.

With one foot in the water, Abram was about to commit his final steps when a snap, a hissing sound, cut the air in two.

At first Abram didn't understand. Looking up, he realized what had happened. The wire stays on the fourth funnel had broken. With the stern nearly level, the funnel wasn't going to fall forward. Rather the water was forcing it back. It was going to crush him.

Abram yelled to warn the others. They were gone.

But out of the corner of his eye, he saw a light reflecting off the ocean's surface.

Bartlett and Second Officer Blair had returned. They were fighting to keep their lifeboat close.

Before Abram could call to them, a surge of water threw Abram from his feet. The funnel smashed onto the deck inches away, throwing him clear of the ship but pushing him deep into the utter darkness of the sea. With hard strokes, feet kicking, he tried to find the surface. Fighting the suction of water from the ship, he wasn't even sure what was up or down. He dared not take a breath but feared his lungs would soon gasp for whatever they could.

He couldn't get above the debris falling around him, hitting him, pulling at him, dragging him down. When a tangle of cables and ropes caught his leg, his body convulsing for air, he knew the wreck was taking him with it. Even so, he felt like he was being drawn upward by angels and saints, just like the day of the fire. No. Not the fire. The launch. The three men. Taking hold of him. Drawing him to the surface. Leading him to whatever holy or unholy place they'd come from.

It seemed forever before they stopped. Other hands grabbed him now, his cold, limp body bumping and scraping against something solid. He heard a thump as he landed on a hard and uneven surface.

For a moment, he lay there. Hazy faces looked down at him.

"Captain Bartlett?"

"You're one lucky son of a bitch," Bartlett said.

Sitting in the safety of the lifeboat, blankets around his shoulders and legs, Abram looked back. The ship's stern was rising out of the water again, lifting higher and nearing the perpendicular, a monolith rising from the ocean. Perhaps her keel still held the two pieces of the ship together, the force of the descent eventually twisting and severing her steel spine. There was no longer any suction. The great ship simply disappeared. Barely a ripple disturbed the surface as the water closed over her huge propeller ... and the last of *Titan's Sister*.

An eerie calm settled over the ocean. Quiet. Peaceful. The night perfectly clear. No moon rising to guide them. No shooting stars for them to pin their hopes on. Abram wondered how nature could be so cruel, so cold, as to remain unaffected by this momentous tragedy.

Someone touched his shoulder. It was Melika. She'd transferred into the captain's boat. She pointed to Abram's hand.

Abram was still clutching Janus's gun, a Colt nine-millimeter semi-automatic. He turned it over in his palm while Melika and Captain Bartlett watched. He looked back at the empty ocean and tossed the weapon overboard. Another piece of debris to litter the ocean floor. Thirteen miles west of *Titanic*'s final resting place. A new grave, covered with a light, silvery blanket of Janus's sand, a platinum shroud. How fitting for such an elegant, formidable ship.

Melika pointed to the horizon. "Look at that," she said.

Drifting south and to the east was a lone lifeboat, one of the collapsibles Janus had freed. It was barely visible in the dark, distinguishable only by a lantern set on the forward staff. A slight haze, perhaps vestiges of steam from the descending ship, encircled the small vessel, the vapor guiding the collapsible home to *Titanic* and the souls who rested there.

At first, Abram thought the boat was empty. Then he saw another light. And another. Three in all, carried by honorable men. He knew who they were. Their foray into the present had altered their images. But Abram could see with 20/20 hindsight now. Thomas Andrews, J. Bruce Ismay, Edward Smith. The shipbuilder, owner, and captain.

Their lanterns shed light on others.

A young woman holding an infant in her arms. An African American couple and their son, the mother looking so much like Melika. And Blake, Abram's friend.

Victims of fate.

Faces of understanding. Faces of peace.

All but one.

In their midst, sitting with his head lowered, was a man weary and forlorn. A man who'd built the stage where this disaster had played out. It was Janus.

Abram glanced at Melika. If she saw anything other than the lone lifeboat, she didn't say.

But she took his hand.

"I'm sorry I doubted you, Abram," she said.

"It's okay." He tightened his grip around hers. "It's all good now."

Watching the lifeboat begin its thirteen-mile journey to *Titanic*'s wreck, Abram wasn't surprised that the haze broadened as more lifeboats joined in, those from the *Sister*, yet stenciled with *Titanic*'s name. Tiny vessels, each with a lantern at the bow, each heading back to where they belonged, all of them carrying the burden for those who couldn't help asking why and what if? Victims of tragedy, taking with them the guilt of those who had survived. Leaving the past to finally rest in peace.

Bartlett turned to his men.

His voice was low, confident. "All right, crew. Let's get underway. Officer at the helm, steer west by southwest."

The sudden movement of the boat caught Melika and Abram off guard. To keep from falling, they grabbed each other, a tight embrace.

Bartlett, the staid, calm commander who'd saved them all, chuckled. "Hey, you two," he said. "Don't rock the boat."

Melika smiled at Abram. "A little late for that."

978-0-595-45961-2
0-595-45961-7

Printed in the United States
109496LV00002B/19/P